WILD DOGS

The Wolves, Coyotes, and Foxes of North America

by Erwin A. Bauer

Photographs by Erwin and Peggy Bauer
Foreword by John Madson

CHRONICLE BOOKS

SAN FRANCISCO

This book is dedicated to the Sierra Club, the Wilderness Society, Defenders of Wildlife, the National Parks and Conservation Association, the Montana Wilderness Association, The National Audubon Society, the National Wildlife Federation, Friends of McNeil River, the Jackson Hole Alliance, the Greater Yellowstone Coalition, and other organizations that have worked to save wild dogs and their environment.

Printed in Hong Kong.

Book and cover designed by David Alcorn.
Maps designed by Eureka Cartography.

Library of Congress Cataloging-in-Publication Data

Bauer, Erwin A.
     Wild dogs : the wolves, coyotes, and foxes of North America / text by Erwin A. Bauer ; photographs by Erwin and Peggy Bauer.
         p.   cm.
     ISBN 0-8118-0690-1 (hc). – ISBN 0-8118-0405-4 (pbk.)
     1. Wolves—North America. 2. Coyotes—North America. 3. Foxes—North America. I. Title.
QL737.C22B38 1994
599.74′442—dc20   93-29205
                                                        CIP

Distributed in Canada by Raincoast Books,
112 East Third Avenue, Vancouver, B.C. V5T 1C8

10 9 8 7 6 5 4 3 2 1

Chronicle Books
275 Fifth Street
San Francisco, CA 94103

Contents

Foreword
by John Madson

I t has been said that Joe Bauer's long experience with North American mammals dates back to when he came across the Bering Land Bridge with many of them. This, of course, is a slight exaggeration. But there's no denying the fact that in terms of total mileage, and nearly half a century's production of quality words and photographs, no outdoor communicator in the world can really match Joe Bauer. ("Erwin" is used only in bylines or by strangers.)

I heard recently that Joe and Peggy just made their twentieth trip to Africa—and that's not a patch on their myriad journeys into the mountains, deserts, swamps, forests, and arctic of North America. None of this travel has been idle tourism. It is always geared to production—to photographing and documenting wild creatures and wild places. In the course of this they have often met foxes, wolves, or coyotes. Sometimes they were the objects of a particular quest; often they were met while searching out something else, such as the egg-eating arctic fox seen as Joe was suspended over an Alaskan cliff while photographing a colony of murres. However such encounters occurred, they are rich parts of the Bauers' experience. Ours too, since this book is a result.

Opposite: Unlike many other species of wild dog, the gray fox is an omnivore.

Few North Americans will ever see a gray wolf in the wild; fewer still, an arctic fox. Some of us have had the luck to see the lovely red-orange of a red fox against a snowy hillside, and to see and hear coyotes in the West. Generally, such wild dogs are jealous of their privacy and have the intelligence and skill to guard it. Coyotes and foxes have survived our persecutions, by and large, and have even flourished. After all, they are consummate professionals in the art of survival.

When I was a boy growing up in central Iowa, full of the trigger-itch, the red fox was a prized trophy. Reynard was not only elusive and hard to kill, but *needed* killing. After all, he often took the pheasants and rabbits that *I* wanted! His beautiful pumpkin-colored pelt stood for three things: the hunter's degree of skill, a $10 check from the fur dealer, and the removal of a hated predator from our tame farmscapes. Such was my training.

My education began one early summer morning when I was bounty hunting groundhogs, and I stopped at the edge of a timbered bluff that rose above a small alfalfa field that often produced a woodchuck. As I lay just inside the trees, watching, a vixen red fox came out of the riverside thicket, followed by four pups. I carefully eased my rifle into position, waiting for her to come a bit closer.

She, too, was hunting. And teaching, as well. Back arched, ears pricked forward, she began

making little stiff-legged leaps through the alfalfa, then suddenly pouncing and tossing a mouse high into the air. There would be a puppyish scramble for the prize, the mother fox watching carefully, and then the class would move on a few yards. This went on for perhaps half an hour until the little family melted back into the heavy cover. Only then did I realize that the vixen had been well within the range of my forgotten rifle. The pups had learned something that morning. So had I. And the memory has been an infinitely finer trophy than the vixen's thin summer pelt would have been.

Not long ago, the public attitude toward our native wild hunters was the same sort of blind adolescent prejudice with which I grew up. Migrating raptors were still being shot by the thousands on the infamous Hawk Mountain in Pennsylvania, hawks and owls were unprotected in every state, and the old Bureau of Biological Survey was tireless in its persecution of cougars, coyotes, and wolves. Red and gray foxes were bountied in many states.

But we're slowly maturing, beginning to realize that there are places in our world for animals such as cougars, foxes, wolves, and coyotes—places that can be filled by nothing else, and which would be achingly empty if such creatures were hunted and poisoned into oblivion. Ranchers and farmers have told me that this shift in attitude is due to urbaniza-

tion and loss of realistic contact with the land, with a resultant romanticizing of wild predators. "Let 'em try to raise sheep in coyote country and they'd damn quick change their minds!" such stockmen say. And there's some truth in that. But it's also true that many urbanites have learned to perceive these predators as biological indicators of quality natural environments. They embody the "spirit of place" as much as any wild creatures. Subtract the coyote from a prairie slope, the wolf from a stretch of tundra, and the fox from a farm woodlot, and those places are the poorer for it. They lose a measure of their vital essence and can never be the same again.

Since that long-ago morning when I watched the red vixen teaching her pups to hunt, I've met a great many foxes and coyotes and heard the wolf song from Isle Royale to the north slope of Alaska's Brooks Range. Each encounter deepens my respect for these wild dogs of North America—and for the skill and dedication of photographer-writers like Joe and Peggy Bauer. Professionals all, keeping the faith.

J.M.

∎

Above: In Alaska, a gray wolf wades through a stream in search of salmon.

Introduction

Late one golden summer afternoon I was sitting on our back porch savoring sundown as it painted the magnificent Montana landscape. To the south I could see the broad Paradise Valley through which the Yellowstone River descends from the national park. Looming just to the east and only a short hike away is the Absaroka range of the Rocky Mountains and the Absaroka-Beartooth Wilderness. Much closer to our home was an extensive backyard colony of Richardson ground squirrels, which early each June becomes a zone of constant noisy activity. As I watched, a dozen or more squirrels grazed, wrestled, and dug dens all around. Only a few feet away a litter of young squirrels play-fought in a clump of feathery sage.

Suddenly, all the bustle stopped and everything was quiet. Next thing I knew not a single ground squirrel was in sight anywhere. Soon I spotted the reason: a badger was slowly approaching the colony with a coyote following a few feet behind. Long ago coyotes learned how much easier it is to capture ground squirrels if they hunt with badgers.

As soon as the badger reached the outer limit of the squirrel colony, it halted abruptly and began

digging. Clods of earth flew as the digger slowly disappeared underground. Very alert now, the coyote maneuvered closer then sprang forward. In an instant the wild dog was loping away with a squirrel in its jaws (see photos on page 80). Neither the badger nor any of the squirrels reappeared before dark.

What I had witnessed was a remarkable partnership that has evolved over time between two unrelated carnivores. For most of the year, ground squirrels hibernate in deep burrows, emerging each spring to graze on fresh green grass and forbs (weeds). At the same time their young are born. Being very active and visible, the newborn squirrels are important prey for every predator from hawks and eagles to foxes and coyotes all with their own ravenous young to feed.

This strange partnership probably began like this: A badger's sense of smell and hearing are keen enough to detect ground squirrels, gophers, or prairie dogs in underground dens. Badgers are also muscular enough to dig down quickly to corner victims where they live. But dens usually have other entrances—escape routes—and many a fleeing squirrel is nabbed above ground by an opportunist coyote.

While it is tempting to anthropomorphize and conclude this is an example of friendship between wild

Above: A female gray wolf takes a drink from a pool of water before joining her family for a hunt.

species, instead it is strictly a convenience. Biologists Steve and Kathy Minta, who studied badgers intensively at the National Elk Refuge in Wyoming, concluded the coyotes weren't the only benefactors. They believe badgers must also gain something from the partnership because they at least tolerate the presence of these canids, with occasionally two or three coyotes living off the badger's labor. This is one of the best examples I know of the acute intelligence and adaptability characteristic of all wild dogs.

Coyotes, like badgers and all wild carnivores, are decended from a common ancestor. About thirty-five million years ago *Hesperocyon* (the earliest, or dawn, dog), descended from the treetop world of its ancestors. Dawn dog had a long tail and low-slung body that could pass easily beneath dense undergrowth, enabling the animal to dig and to live close to the ground. As a carnivore, dawn dog had sharp teeth designed to slash as well as crunch on a mixed diet of small mammals, beetles, grubs, and fruit. From the beginning, it was an opportunist.

Over the next ten million years or so, dawn dog gradually divided—evolved—into five separate families. One of these, *Amphicyonidae* (half dogs), disappeared from the earth six million years ago. The other surviving families are *Mustelidae* (weasels, minks, otters, and badgers), *Procyonidae* (raccoons and their allies), *Ursidae* (bears), and *Canidae* (wild dogs).

Today the wild dog family contains thirty-five different species, ranging from the tiny fennec and the much larger, spotted hunting dogs of Africa to the dholes of Asia and the almost unknown bush dogs of the Amazon basin. Eight of these species of wild dogs live in North America: gray and red wolves; coyotes; and red, gray, kit, swift, and Arctic foxes. At least one other American wild dog, the dire wolf, became extinct long ago and we know of its existence only through a skeleton recovered from the La Brea Tar Pits in Los Angeles.

Above: Two gray fox pups play by their den entrance.

Dogs were probably the first animals ever domesticated and have remained man's allies throughout recorded history. They have been bred and trained to be useful as well as to be companions. Most dogs bear little resemblance to the gray wolf from which they likely descended. Some domestic breeds are twice the size of the largest wild dogs; others are tiny. Some have long, luxuriant coats; others are nearly hairless. Few have retained any of the qualities of their wild ancestors.

However all North American wild dogs do share common traits and physiques. They are shy and elusive, with acute senses of sight, smell, and hearing. They share generally slender bodies with bushy tails, erect ears, piercing eyes, and long slender muzzles, altogether presenting a lean and hungry appearance. All are far more robust than they seem at first glance. Wild dogs cool themselves by panting with open mouths and lolling tongues that allow for rapid reduction of excess body heat.

Modern-day wild dogs stand upright on all four legs, rather than crouching or slinking. Their paws are distinctive, having five toes on each forefoot and four with nonretractable nails on the hind foot. The fifth front toe or dewclaw is on the inside of the foot above the pad. All wild dogs can travel fast and for long distances.

Wild dogs' teeth are as distinctive as their feet, their long legs, and their body posture. Each type has forty-two teeth—twenty on top and twenty-two below. Most noticeable are the four large canine teeth, or tusks, at the front corners of the mouth, ideal for killing and tearing prey apart. Behind the canines are rows of premolars and, farthest back, molars. The last premolar of the upper jaw and the first molar below it are called carnassial teeth, also used to tear flesh. Molars are the grinders dogs use for chewing.

All North American wild canids produce a single litter every year of two to a dozen pups. The young are unable to hunt or to care for themselves for a period ranging from several weeks to several months. These long periods of dependency seem to develop strong social or family ties.

Wild dogs demonstrate many behaviors that should endear them to humans. Both males and females are dedicated to tending pups, in marked contrast to male wild cats. One explanation for the difference is that unlike cats, dogs eat a varied, omnivorous diet (fruit, insects, carrion, small vertebrates) that allows two or more dogs to feed side by side without conflict. This abundance of food choices might also encourage cohabitation within a territory and thus promote closer links between parents and young. Although some wild dogs are solitary and others highly social, all are mostly monogamous.

Their tails are an indicator of mood: dogs hold them erect when playing, or when they are well fed, or otherwise contented. They wag their tails to seek acceptance or express pleasure. A tail tucked beneath the hind legs indicates fear or uncertainty.

Whenever food is available wild dogs gorge themselves, sometimes even to stupefaction, but are able to survive long periods with little or no food.

Scarcely a decade after wading ashore in the New World, the Pilgrims of Massachusetts declared a bounty on wolves, which they felt threatened their personal safety and their livestock. They feared wolves as much as they did the brooding, primeval forests. In contrast, the Native Americans of New England had always respected wolves.

Today over half of the world's wild dog species are either threatened or endangered. That is also true in North America, where the plight of gray and red wolves and kit and swift foxes is of great concern.

What we have is a paradox. On one side, the wild dog is the ancestor of man's best friend, the playmate of our children, guardian of our homes, and faithful ally on hunting trips. On the other, we have spent literally billions of dollars trying to eradicate the animal that ate Little Red Riding Hood's grandma. While those efforts have all but eliminated some species from much of their range, that same persecution has spurred other wild dogs to evolve into even more resourceful, adaptable, and clever survivors.

Make no mistake about wild dogs: their survival is important, if not critical, to everyone. Not only do these highly interesting animals belong in our world, they also furnish us with an accurate report of how well man is treating the environment. When at night we can hear the bark of a fox or the wail of a coyote, the land out there is in a lot better condition than if all were silent.

■

Above: Sibling rivalry for two gray wolf pups erupts in midwinter, when prey is scarce.

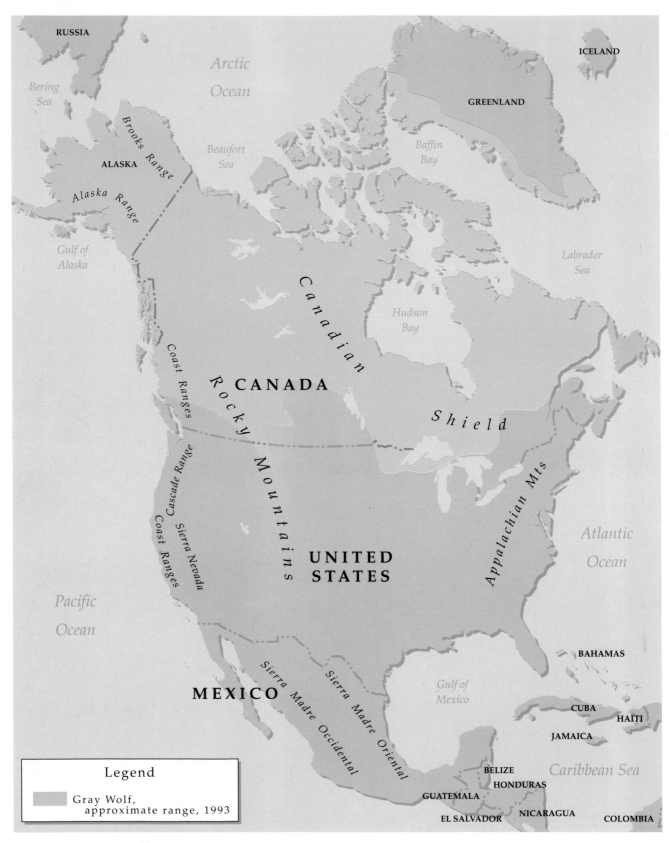

Legend

Gray Wolf, approximate range, 1993

Range of the gray wolf.

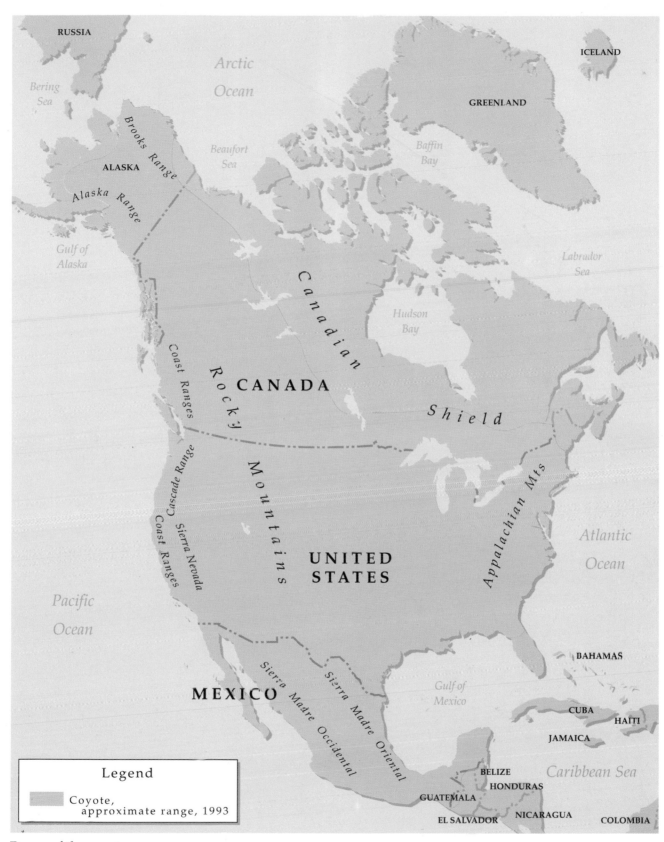

Arctic
Ocean

Bering
Sea

GREENLAND

Brooks Range

ALASKA

Beaufort
Sea

Baffin
Bay

Alaska Range

Gulf of
Alaska

Canadian

Labrador
Sea

Hudson
Bay

Coast Ranges

CANADA

Shield

Rocky

Cascade Range

Coast Ranges

Sierra Nevada

Mountains

UNITED
STATES

Appalachian Mts

Atlantic
Ocean

Pacific

Ocean

BAHAMAS

Sierra Madre Occidental

Sierra Madre Oriental

MEXICO

Gulf of
Mexico

CUBA

HAITI

JAMAICA

Caribbean Sea

BELIZE

HONDURAS

GUATEMALA

EL SALVADOR

NICARAGUA

COLOMBIA

Legend
Coyote, approximate range, 1993

Range of the coyote.

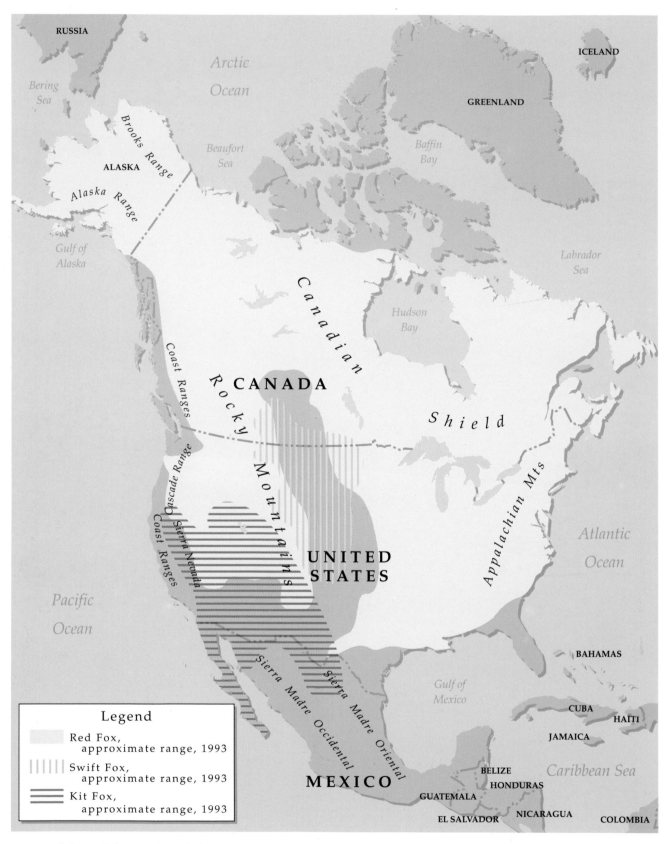

Range of the red, kit, and swift fox.

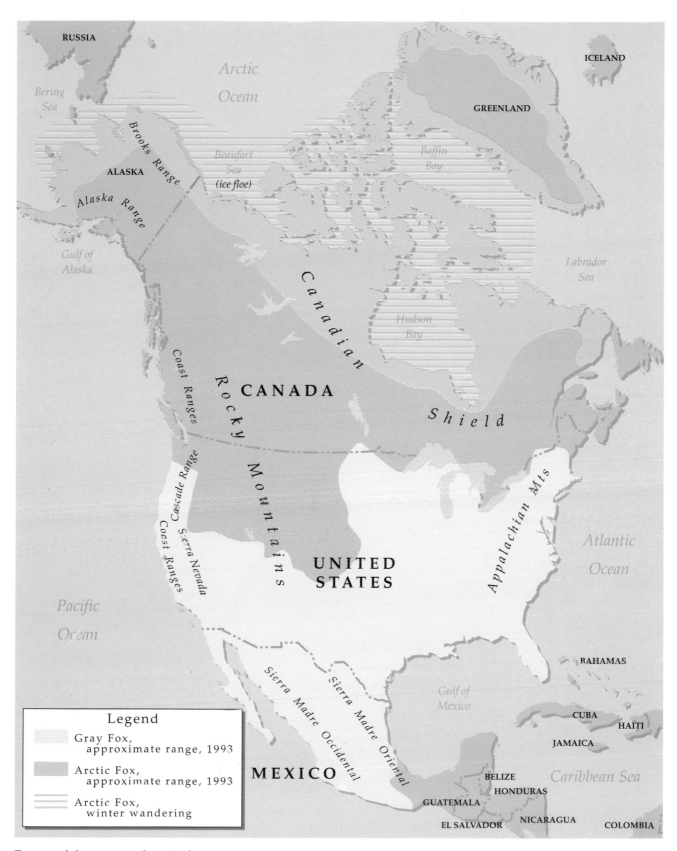

Range of the gray and arctic fox.

Gray wolves howl for a number of reasons: to maintain communication, to call the roll of pack members, and to declare their presence in a territory. Each wolf has a distinctive voice that other pack members recognize immediately. Most howling is done at night.

WOLVES

In August 1992, Peggy and I joined a Canadian Rivers Expedition to explore the entire 185-mile length of Canada's Alsek River. Only one or two other groups had preceded us down this almost unknown waterway through one of the largest intact wilderness areas left on earth. The trip began in Kluane National Park, Yukon, crossed the northernmost tip of British Columbia, skirted the crumbling faces of living glaciers, and passed through Glacier Bay National Park, Alaska, to end at Dry Bay on the Gulf of Alaska. Almost wherever we stepped ashore to hike, gather firewood, or pitch overnight camps, we found fresh tracks of gray wolves and grizzly bears. Clearly both species were fairly abundant in that remote region, where so few humans had ever set foot.

Although we counted thirty-three grizzly bears, almost three for every day on the river, some at close range, we did not have even the briefest glimpse of a wolf. That made me ponder again the intelligence and shyness of this animal, the largest of the world's wild dogs. I wondered how many of them had watched us floating by in our inflatable rafts.

Ever since an early summer morning in 1960 on another wild river, the American in Alaska's Katmai National Park (then a national monument), I have been a serious wolf watcher and photographer. What drew me to Katmai, though, were the brown bears and the salmon fishing. I caught plenty of the latter and saw large numbers of the former while fishing. But what really fascinated me was the family of five wolves that came to the river near our camp every evening to participate in the salmon bonanza.

The wolves were not nearly as efficient anglers as the brown bears, and seemed to expend a lot more energy just to capture a sockeye or red salmon that had finished spawning and was dying in shallow water. But the wolves were persistent. In time, they became very curious about me: one pure-white animal would sit for hours, half hidden in vegetation directly across the current, staring toward my tent. One morning it crossed the river for a closer look before disappearing into an alder thicket. Probably as much as any other animal, that one wolf ignited my lifelong interest in wild dogs. Now I wonder even more why we saw no wolves at all along the Alsek.

Only two hundred years ago *Canis lupus* (the gray, tundra, or timber wolf) was the most widely distributed mammal on earth. Absent only from deserts, rain forests, and the highest alpine zones, wolves roamed everywhere across North America, Europe, and northern Asia. They still survive wherever the northern hemisphere wilderness remains largely unsettled, but everywhere else they have been driven out by civilization. In North America wolves have been completely eradicated from the entire United States, except for Alaska and small populations in northern Minnesota, Michigan's Isle Royale National Park, and western Montana.

Gradually, wolves seem to be moving southward from the vicinity of Glacier National Park, Montana, as if on course toward Yellowstone Park. As I write this, six or seven packs seem fairly well established in our state. There is a chance that we might even see or hear them one day here in Paradise Valley.

Gray wolves are gone from the heavily developed territory across southern Canada, but packs still roam freely across northern Canada all the way from Labrador to Yukon Territory. I have seen them as far south as Prince Albert National Park in Saskatchewan, Riding Mountain National Park in Manitoba, and in all the Rocky Mountain national parks of Alberta, including Waterton Lakes on the Montana border.

Taxonomists generally agree that once in North America there were twenty-one gray wolf subspecies, with differences that were minor and usually undetectable to the eye. But most of them are gone. The prairie or buffalo wolves that followed and lived off the great bison herds survive if at all only in scattered captive groups. It is unlikely there are any Mexican wolves alive in the wild, although there are several small captive populations that might someday be reintroduced into a suitable habitat.

The gray wolf is not an easy animal to describe. Its basic colors are white, gray, and black, but usually there is great variation in shading even within a family or pack. Arctic wolves tend to be white or nearly white, but a pack might include individuals that are buff, brownish, or even almost black. Where snow covers the ground for much of the year, a white pelage is a distinct advantage; the farther south a wolf lives and the more wooded (versus open tundra) its environment, the darker it is likely to be. The color of some wolves even changes slightly with age, and when an adult wolf molts in spring, losing its long guard hairs, it is much lighter in appearance. Many wolves have distinct color patterns, such as a dark stripe down the back or a dark mane on a light individual or a silvery mane on a dark wolf that gives it a grizzled look. In truth, the gray wolf is not necessarily "gray" at all.

As with all animals that are actively disliked, feared, or hunted as trophies, the wolf's size is often exaggerated. Average size varies as much as fur color, but everywhere males are larger than females. Northern wolves tend to be larger than those farther south. A fully grown northern male will stand almost three feet at the shoulder and measure six feet or so from nose to tip of extended tail. Males weigh from 125 to 150 pounds. Small females from southern populations may reach only 65 or 70 pounds by the time they are old enough to breed.

The largest wolf ever recorded was a 197-pound male shot in central Alaska, near Mount McKinley. Contrast that size to a healthy male German shepherd, which weighs only half as much. A wild wolf also has longer legs, a narrower chest, and a more graceful body than any shepherd.

Although no other wild animal looks exactly like a gray wolf, an inexperienced observer might mistake a very small wolf for a very large coyote. But a wolf's muzzle is always larger and it runs with its tail stretched out straight behind. However, the only certain way to distinguish a wolf from a coyote or from a domestic dog or wolf-dog hybrid, is by skull size and dimensions. The jaws are larger and the brain case smaller in a wolf skull than in a coyote skull. Wolves also have more massive teeth than coyotes or domestic dogs of any size.

One reason we may not see wolves very often, even where there are sizable wolf populations, is that most of their activity is at night or at twilight. The cooler the weather, the likelier wolves are to hunt and move about during daylight. I have been lucky enough to hear them howling many times, but only twice, both times well after sunrise and on foggy, misty mornings, did I ever actually see one howling. I have heard African lions roar and the hacksaw cough of leopards just outside my safari tent, but neither of these is as haunting, as unsettling, as the savage symphony of gray wolves on a cold, still, northern night.

There are many theories about wolf howls, including the one that suggests they simply enjoy it. More likely the howl is a means of communicating among pack members as well as a warning to intruders in the howler's territory. Calling could be a form of bonding or a family roll call when members are separated or a way to coax stragglers and young animals to keep up with a traveling pack. Just as each wolf has its own distinctive odor, each also has a unique voice other wolves can identify.

No doubt the easiest place to observe North American wolves today is in Denali National Park, Alaska, where the animals have not been hunted for seventy-six years. As a result many wolves there pay almost no attention to the humans they encounter hiking or aboard buses shuttling along the single park road. Wolves are credited with being far more

Above, left and below: This sibling pair of young wolves, seven to eight months old, have captured a striped skunk. After gnawing, fighting over the carcass, and rolling on the ground near it, they return to an adult, probably the mother, as if for approval. Finally, they drink in a nearby pond.

capable, efficient killers than they really are. A pack of wolves does not just select its prey, run it down, kill it, then begin to eat it before it is dead. Plenty of physical effort is expended, and thousands of footprints are left behind for every meal obtained. Life is hard in a wolf pack. Two weeks may pass between kills—and substantial meals. A hungry pack of fifteen has been known to completely consume a four-hundred-pound moose, or about twenty pounds of meat each, in just twenty-four hours.

During several summer and fall trips to Denali we have seen wolves fail when hunting far more often than they succeed. Soon after daybreak during a summer trip there, not far from the Teklanika public campground, Peggy and I saw a single wolf attack a young bull moose, by ripping and tearing at its hindquarters. The moose escaped the initial assault by wading into the Teklanika River, where the current was so deep and swift that the wolf was unable to maintain a leghold, and could not follow. The moose was safe as long as it remained standing in the numbingly cold water.

This wolf-moose standoff lasted all day, through the short sub-Arctic night, and throughout a second day. As long as the moose stayed in the river, the wolf would lie down nearby watching it; sometimes it even seemed to fall asleep. But whenever that moose tried to leave the river, the wolf renewed its attack. Once, hanging onto the nose of the moose, the wolf was dragged into the Teklanika until it kicked free and resumed its waiting game (see photos page 37).

But the moose weakened noticeably and eventually collapsed sometime during the second night. The carcass was washed far downstream before grounding on a gravel bar, where the killer found it a second time. Wolves may be more persistent hunters than they are efficient. This doggedness is well illustrated by wolves' ability to travel; they spend about a third of their adult life on the move.

Over open terrain, running wolves have been clocked at up to twenty-eight miles per hour in short runs (up to two hundred yards), and at about twenty-two miles per hour for runs of a mile or two. But that is not really fast compared to their hooved animal prey. What wolves can do is lope smoothly for hours on end, almost without effort or changing pace. One August morning in Denali we encountered an adult female wolf trotting steadily along the road near Sable Pass. Two hours later we met the animal again. It had covered eighteen miles and was still going along at about nine miles per hour.

Stranger still, we met that female a third time that same day. I was photographing a large bull moose just shedding its antler velvet at the onset of the rut. With camera and telephoto lens mounted on a tripod and focused on the moose, I glanced to the side and there stood the now-familiar white wolf, staring directly at my subject. Other than to turn directly toward the wolf, the moose made no move whatsoever to run away, or to charge. In the moment it took me to shift the camera angle to try to capture both animals in the viewfinder, the wolf was gone.

Many scientists have studied wolves in North America, but none for so long or with such intensity as biologist L. David Mech. He began his first investigations in 1957 in Isle Royale, Michigan. Since then he has flown in light aircraft the equivalent of three times around the world, tracking wolf packs and collecting data. Add to that the three-thousand-plus miles he has traveled on foot and by boat, snowmobile, and car almost everywhere the largest wild dogs are found on the continent. Mech told me that from all of his experiences he had drawn two main conclusions: First, that an old Siberian proverb, "the wolf is kept fed by its feet," is absolutely true. Second, wolves are by no means the craven relentless killers they are so often claimed to be. During one study, when Mech followed a pack of 15 for 400 hours in a small ski plane, the wolves encountered 131 moose, but managed to take only seven—only those moose least able to escape through speed, strength, or endurance; in other words, the youngest, the oldest, and the weakest.

Mech's four decades of diligent work has revealed much, maybe even most, of what we know about wolves today. By radio-collaring more than two hundred animals, he discovered that northern Minnesota packs require territories of from fifty to one hundred square miles each. The boundaries are established by scent marking, urine, and by howling. (Other pilot researchers found that packs in Alaska have much larger territories, up to five thousand square miles.) One lone male wolf Mech tagged, not a member of a pack, covered 129 miles on a straight line in a single journey. The range of loners may be greater than packs because they must travel cautiously along the edges of established pack territories to avoid being killed. Except for people and parasites, wolves are their own greatest natural enemies.

To prosper, even to survive anywhere, wolves require not only large tracts of wilderness, but wilderness that supports adequate prey. Prairies and open foothills populated by bison, in the days before all of those areas were converted to ranchlands for cattle, were ideal. Arctic tundra with caribou herds and musk-oxen, or mixed forests, meadows, and

Left and below: These young wolves, brown in color and three to four weeks old, emerge from their natal den, possibly for their first look outside, where they are nursed by the mother. The mother tries to enlarge the den when it becomes difficult to pick up the pups and carry them back inside.

wetlands with moose and deer are all suitable habitats. Gray wolves do not exist in any numbers in vast unbroken evergreen forests, where there is little understory for hooved prey to browse. Nor can wolves live for long in areas of deep winter snow because travel and hunting are difficult and most prey migrates elsewhere anyway.

Their prey dictates the wolves' social structure and the way they must live in well-organized packs. While a single wolf had difficulty bringing down that young, possibly unhealthy, moose I described, a pack would have less trouble with even a larger animal. Although it may have to locate and test many moose to find a vulnerable one, the odds favor a pack over a loner in pressing an attack and making a kill. There is always danger when hunting powerful, formidable prey, and pack members are often injured by flying hooves or flailing antlers with the older and least experienced wolves most likely to be hurt, sometimes fatally.

Hunting in packs is doubly important in summer when wolves are raising their young because a litter of several pups may need more nutrition than two parents alone can provide. The pack is also a kind of social insurance for older and disabled members, which sometimes remain with the pack and are fed along with the pups. Often these members are rejected and become camp followers, finishing off the scant remains of abandoned kills.

A pack maintains its structure and cohesion in many ways, two of which are howling and scent. The strong bonds between mated pairs, juvenile submission to adults, patterns of dominance and subordination all contribute toward making a wolf pack work. Pack size usually increases or decreases according to the amount of prey available. If a pack's numbers grow beyond the habitat's capacity to feed all of its members, domestic violence breaks out within the pack.

Depending on latitude, females come into estrus once a year between January and April, which is when mating occurs. The southernmost wolves breed earliest. Almost always only the alpha pair, or dominant male and female in a pack, mate. As with all canids, mating consists of a copulatory session that lasts as long as thirty minutes. Young are born nine weeks later. Litter sizes range from only one pup in bad times to a dozen when prey is abundant, with six being average. The pups are born in burrows or natural caves, beneath deadfalls, or in other concealed spots. One Yukon female gave birth to a litter of five in the hibernation den of a grizzly bear that was vacated only weeks earlier. A female may use the same den year after year. I saw such a den in Labrador where a pile of crisscrossed tree trunks had been deposited by a river changing its course.

Opposite and above: This young pup, apparently the most adventurous of its litter, explores the vicinity of the den. At this age the pups are most vulnerable to predators like bears and wolverines.

Mothers remain at the den nursing the helpless, slate-colored pups for about two months, all the while being fed by other pack members. After two months the young are moved away to what might be called rendezvous, near which they remain and where they are fed until they are strong enough to travel with the pack. Living at the rendezvous the pups are most vulnerable to predation by bears, wolverines, or other wolves, either loners or members of rival packs, so sometimes an older pack member stays behind to guard them. During this time the pups begin to venture farther and farther from the site, exploring and at the same time establishing their rank within the litter through intense play-fighting. At six months the average pup weighs fifty to sixty pounds.

Some young remain with their pack permanently, a few eventually becoming alpha breeders. But most leave to try to find their own territories before they are two years old. Females are sexually mature at two and males a year later, but this is no guarantee they will be able to breed because mating within a pack is restricted to and suppressed by the alpha pair.

Mech learned that Minnesota wolves might live as long as thirteen years, with the rare female still producing pups at eleven, but the average lifespan is probably less than half that. Besides the toll taken by humans and other wolves, hunting injuries, starva-tion during bitter winters, disease, and parasites also limit longevity. From time to time there have been sudden, drastic regional die-offs of Alaskan wolves from canine distemper, possibly contracted from sled dogs in the area. During the early 1990s there was a drastic and mysterious die-off of wolves on Isle Royale. Even now, the exact cause remains unknown. Arthritis, discovered when examining wolf carcasses, may be a more serious problem than most biologists suspect because it can greatly hamper a wolf attacking a larger animal. Parasites are responsible for a sometimes high mortality in wolf pups.

Rabies can be a terrible killer, too. Native Americans recognized the disease among buffalo wolves long ago and feared it. Yellowed journals of the early 1800s contain records of rabid wolves entering encampments and attacking dogs, cattle, and people. In 1874, a rabid wolf invaded an army post on the Arkansas River and ran amok among privates, corporals, officers, and their wives before being shot by a sentinel. Several troops died painfully from "hydrophobia," now known as rabies.

Above: As they grow older and stronger, gray wolf pups explore farther and farther from their den or pack rendezvous. These pups are between two and three months old. Sometimes a pack member remains nearby to guard them while the others hunt, but increasingly the pups are left alone.

Opposite: A six-month-old gray wolf pup lies panting in the hot afternoon sun.

Many misconceptions persist about wolves as predators. For example, they do not always use the same hunting strategies. Each day brings a new game of wits. Some prey might require wearing down in a long chase. But capturing a white-tailed deer might mean cornering or surrounding the swift animal, or driving it out into a lake in summer or onto a pond with a thinly frozen surface in winter. Another myth is that wolves slaughter large numbers of helpless prey at one time out of blood lust. Not only would that be too exhausting, it would also decimate their food supply, which must be sustained.

Even seemingly helpless deer fawns have a defense—in numbers. All young whitetails are dropped at about the same time of year, so this annual bonanza for wolves lasts only a short time. The fawns soon develop enough speed and agility to outrun the predators.

Whenever wolves capture an animal large enough to last more than one meal, they gorge to repletion. Usually, they move away some distance, sometimes more than a mile, to rest and digest before consuming the remains. Only in areas where they are likely to be disturbed or are especially wary of humans will a pack desert a certain food source for the uncertainty of hunting again.

Occasionally, wolves cache uneaten parts of a carcass to save it from other packs or scavengers or to feed pups. In Denali Park we once saw a young female carrying a haunch of moose calf for more than a mile before she disappeared into dense vegetation near Wonder Lake. At times wolves will hide meat in shallow depressions, which they then hastily cover over with earth. As often as not the cache is found by wolverines, bears, foxes, eagles, or ravens before the wolves can return to it.

During the 1800s when Americans were winning (or more likely losing) the West, no creature inspired more tales both true and fanciful than "rogue" wolves. Like some of the notorious man- and cattle-killing grizzly bears, "outlaw" gray wolves did exist wherever sheep, goats, and cattle were being introduced on lands they would soon overgraze. With natural prey driven out, wolves naturally turned to mutton and beef. It wasn't as nutritious as deer and antelope, but sheep were easier to catch. For a while wolves probably did

Left: After killing a weakened bull elk, this wolf gorges. The pack will return to feed on the carcass as long as any meat remains. A hungry wolf can eat twenty pounds of meat at one meal.

make raising livestock a losing proposition in Oklahoma and points north.

One Oklahoma wolf named Geronimo devoured fresh mutton from one end of McCurtain County to the other before being run to exhaustion and captured at Broken Bow. Other cattle killers that roamed the Cherokee Nation for a long time before being caught had names like Lucifer, Bloody Lobo, Cedar Canyon King, and (after gnawing its way out of a bear trap) Two Toes. The Osage Phantom of Tulsa County was never caught.

Texas stockmen hired professional hunters and bought and imported the best packs of hounds money could buy to rid the state of surviving wolves. A man named Q. T. Stevens spent a fortune to breed his own pack of wolf hounds and rode vast distances on horseback, eventually wiping out the last elusive, notorious gray wolf pack that roamed the Texas Hill Country. In 1905, President Theodore Roosevelt went wolf hunting in Hardeman County, Texas, accompanied by many curious cowboys and a troop of U.S. cavalry. But he had come too late, whether he realized it or not. The wolves there were already finished.

The last of the famous rogues was Old Aquila, a wolf that ate tens of thousands of dollars worth of beefsteak over eight years. Estimated to weigh 150 pounds and with a heavy price on its head, the best professional hunters and trappers hardly ever had a glimpse of it. No one really knows what happened to Old Aquila except that suddenly the killings in southern Arizona stopped. By 1976, gray wolves were gone from almost every region of the United States between the Canadian and Mexican borders.

For too long no predator has been more hated, feared, and hunted by men than the wolf. The feeling originated in the dread and superstitions of our forbearers and later was heightened by the wolf's role as a cattle killer. At times, primitive and later rural people in eastern Europe were eaten by wolves during plagues and brutal Russian winters. American livestock sometimes met a similar fate. But since the first European settlements in North America there has not been a single recorded wolf attack on a human.

Fortunately, viewpoints are changing. For example, sentiment has been heavily in favor of reintroducing wolves to Yellowstone National Park, where they were deliberately eliminated a half century ago. More and more Americans now regard wolves as fellow residents on a planet in trouble.

■

Opposite: Especially in winter, hunting is almost a full-time necessity. Hunting success is determined by the abundance of prey, weather conditions, and depth and complexion of the snow.

Left and below: In spring and early summer gray wolves of the northern forests often concentrate their hunting along waterways, skirting the shores of lakes, beaver ponds, and streams. Hooved prey like deer and moose are most likely to be found in the lusher vegetation near water. There is also a good chance of capturing beavers, nesting birds, and other small game.

Above: In autumn, wolves of all ages reach their peak physical condition. The body hair grows long and the pelts are sleek in preparation for the winter ahead. Pups now hunt as members of the pack, or at least follow along, and it is no longer necessary for adults to feed them.

Right: Toward the end of a bitter winter the alpha pair of a pack begin a courtship ritual of running, playing, vocalizing, rolling in the snow, sniffing, and licking that ends in mating. At the same time they suppress mating of other members of the pack.

Left and below: A white female pauses to drink from a pool, which is drying up during an autumn dry spell, before joining the family on a hunt through the crisp brown forest.

Above: A young wolf finds the antlers of an old deer kill and carries it away, even though it is meatless. Frequently when there is a surfeit of meat, wolves will cache it. Far too often it is quickly discovered by scavengers.

Opposite: A full-grown healthy gray wolf is an agile, lithe, even graceful hunter, easily able to travel over deadfalls and through thick understory as well as across muskeg or tundra. Additionally, it possesses very keen senses of smell, hearing, and vision.

Previous spread: Especially in areas where there is human encroachment or where they have been hunted, wolves tend to be nocturnal. Their hunting activity begins at dusk and ends at daybreak, (when this photograph was taken). A wolf's vision is probably as good in darkness as in daylight.

Above: Gray wolves are among the greatest marathon runners of all the world's animals. A healthy adult can lope at a steady speed, without pause, for twenty to twenty-five miles at close to ten miles per hour over bare ground or hardened snow, which is much faster than the fastest human long-distance runner. It has been estimated that wolves spend about a third of their lives on the move.

Opposite right: The faces of wolves have been described as cruel, intelligent, crafty, curious, handsome, savage, and sly. Depending on the mood, whether well fed or hungry, young and exuberant or experienced, the countenance of a wolf is all of these.

*Above: Across much of their range,
moose are the principal prey of wolves,
but this moose was probably the victim of
a nighttime collision with a truck. This
pair of hunters found the prize on a cold
winter's dawn near a logging road. In
some remote regions wolves have learned
to patrol logging and mining roads for
any dead animals they find along the
right-of-way.*

Left and below: Denali National Park, Alaska. The lone wolf alternately waited and attacked the young bull moose along the Teklanika River for two days and nights before the moose fell during the second night. In the photograph at left, the wolf hangs onto the moose's nose, but is shaken off. Below, the wolf waits half-asleep on the bank while strength drains from the moose standing in the glacial water.

Opposite and above: Almost everywhere it survives the wolf is a mysterious animal that lurks in shadows of deep wilderness areas and is not often seen by humans who understand it.

Above: Siblings spar in winter when prey is scarce, and starvation is a specter. Al such times discipline and cohesion in wolf packs break down, and violence results.

Opposite: Dark pups still not old or strong enough to join the family pack full time beg for food from adults returning from a hunt. Parents feed young either by regurgitating or by returning with animal heads or haunches. Even some very old wolf pack members may survive by begging from successful hunters.

Opposite and above: To other members of a pack, a wolf's face and body language will indicate dominance or subservience, acceptance or displeasure.

Previous spread: Throughout winter a wolf's hunting success and survival depend on how deep, soft, or compacted the snow cover is. A heavy powdery snowfall will be a disadvantage for a powerful, long-legged mammal like a moose. A shallow snow or compacted surface will help in running down swift prey like white-tail deer. A wolf or wolves racing over newly fallen snow is a beautiful sight.

Above: This Mexican subspecies probably no longer exists in the wild, south of the United States border, where it has long been considered an unwelcome cattle killer. If still surviving, its numbers are surely fewer than twenty.

Opposite: Wolves kill to survive, but they are not the wanton killers of folklore and popular belief. They are at the top of the food chain in the balance of nature.

All these large mammals are important prey for species of wolves in different parts of their range. In most areas of the far north wolves virtually live on the caribou herds (above), depending greatly on the caribou calves when their own pups are still young and helpless. In some areas wolf predation may be the main factor in limiting populations of Dall sheep (right). The two species evolved together thousands of years ago and share many mountain ranges of wild Alaska. Mule deer fawns (below) are easy picking for a brief period in early summer before they develop their running legs.

Elk (above) are in great danger when driven by deep snow from their vast summer ranges to concentrate in smaller wintering areas. Although a healthy, determined adult moose (below) is able to stand off several attackers, this species is still a staple in the diet of northern timber wolves. These predators also preyed on antelope (left) that shared western prairies with the bison, another vulnerable species.

All of these are predatory species, carnivores, in varying degrees of competition with gray wolves. Wolverines (above) will eat any pups they find unguarded and may actually take away carcasses (prey) from single or young wolves. The black bear (right) may not be able to keep the deer carcass on which it sits and feeds if a wolf pack comes along. A young grizzly (top) might make a meal for the same wolf pack that keeps its distance from an older grizzly bear. Wolf-grizzly contests over carcasses are not uncommon where the two species share a range.

Above: A black bear manages a standoff with three wolves (the third not shown here) over its food cache, but at dusk (and with more wolves arriving), finally loses it.

Left: Wherever their ranges overlap, cougars also compete for available food supply, especially for deer and elk. However, these two direct carnivores, wolves and cougars, probably never come into direct confrontation.

51

These coyotes have come upon the carcass of a bison killed by a severe Yellowstone Park winter. The meat sustained many more coyotes than just these two for several days. As many as eleven, most arriving from adjacent family territories, were counted in the vicinity. In the end, only the bare skeleton and skull remained of an animal that had weighed eight hundred pounds on the hoof.

COYOTES

It is easier to understand the coyote if first we consider some cold and depressing statistics. In 1909, at the behest of livestock ranchers and wool growers in the West, Congress first funded a national pest and predator control program that has become a scandal and a disgrace. The program was aimed at all wild meat-eaters from eagles to wolves, but primarily at coyotes. Since the inception of this plan, American tax payers have spent billions of dollars on predator control and the government has employed every conceivable means and tactic to eradicate coyotes, despite growing citizen objections and scientific studies that show the slaughter does far more harm than good.

Hunters and trappers of the U.S. Department of Agriculture's Animal Control Branch (ADC) have used everything from traps, guns, aircraft, and the deadliest poisons to military electronic technology and synthetic hormones (for birth control) to eliminate *Canis latrans* from the American landscape. And the ADC has not worked alone. State governments have participated, too, and almost everywhere stockmen have always shot coyotes on sight.

In 1989, the most recent year for which figures are available, government hunters killed 86,502 coyotes in this country, an increase of ten thousand over the previous year. Even during the economic recession of the early 1990s, when federal funding for any domestic program was difficult to obtain, the

ADC still maintained an army of 350 professional hunters and trappers to kill coyotes. In 1990, Congress approved another $30 million to keep this predator control program going.

One campaign in the institutional war on coyotes deserves special attention. In 1962, the ADC reported killing two hundred thousand predators, including opossums, skunks, badgers, black bears, and cougars, but mainly coyotes, to save a few head of cattle and sheep. That same year, at immense cost, the ADC befouled 3 million acres of overgrazed public and private land in the West with 700 tons of poison and 350,000 lethal gas cartridges to kill rodents (prairie dogs, hares, ground squirrels, gophers, and mice) that stockmen claimed were devouring the grasslands their sheep and cattle needed. If left alone, the coyotes would have recycled the rodents for nothing. It makes you wonder if humans really are at the top of the brain chain. You also have to wonder if coyotes will inherit what is left of the earth after the last human is gone. Despite the billions spent on the costly, cruel, and wasteful predator control projects, coyotes are now more abundant than ever in their long evolution.

Besides just maintaining their numbers in western North America, their original range, coyotes have expanded in all directions, and from the country into more densely populated areas. For example, an estimated three thousand coyotes are permanent residents of Los Angeles, where they dine on vitamin-fortified dog food left out on back porches, drink purified water from swimming pools, and occasionally feast on an unsuspecting pampered house cat. Coyotes have now colonized every state east of the Mississippi River and south to the Gulf of Mexico. They live on Ohio farms and in Kentucky bluegrass, in Chicago, Brooklyn, Houston, Kansas City, and in the Connecticut suburbs. Coyotes are trotting down from Texas and northern Mexico into almost all of Central America except the rain forests. Originally natives of grasslands, coyotes are now found in temperate forests and woodlands, in deserts and swamps, in agricultural lands and sub-alpine habitats, and all the way to the Arctic coast. Wherever wolves have been eliminated, coyotes have quickly filled the void. The only boundaries to coyote country seem to be America's ocean shores.

Belatedly, we may be taking a new look at this remarkable wild dog. Robert Crabtree, a biology professor at Montana State University, leads the host of wildlife researchers who assure us that the overkill of the past has only transformed the coyote into a more adaptable, more prolific creature, maybe even an indestructible species. The continuous persecution has caused whole populations of coyotes to reproduce earlier every year and to bear larger litters to compensate for their losses.

The past eighty years of intense predator control have also changed the coyotes' traditional methods of hunting. Instead of concentrating on the small creatures, from voles to jackrabbits (already in short supply because of overgrazing by ranch stock), they have turned to domestic calves and especially lambs to feed their larger litters. In other words, we have made a minor problem far worse by disrupting the entire social system of one animal. What we have today is not the clever "song dog" of Native American folklore; instead the coyote is a "super dog."

For all its survivability, the super dog is certainly not the large and majestic animal its common image makes it out to be. Average males measure between four and five feet from nose to tip of tail, which is usually drooping, and they stand about two feet at the shoulder. They weigh about thirty pounds; the largest known was about seventy pounds. Females are usually slightly smaller and weigh a little less. When shedding in spring and early summer, the coats of coyotes are on the shaggy side and the animals seem more undernourished than efficient killers. At other times they look sleek and prosperous. In southern parts of their range, coyotes tend to be smaller, more lightly furred, and darker in color

than their northern cousins, which are usually very light. The coyotes I watch most often in Montana are cream- to tan-colored.

America's super dog did not survive its long persecution by being unwary and trusting of people. Rather, they were exactly the opposite. Despite their current abundance and wide range, humans are still more likely to hear than to see coyotes. Yellowstone and Canadian national parks in Alberta, where they have always been protected, are exceptions. In these places they are easier to watch, and it is here that we have spent considerable time photographing them. But even in these sanctuaries, coyotes are best remembered for their haunting songs at dusk, which are difficult to forget or to mistake for any other wild sound. The coyote's howl, more high-pitched yipping than a true howl like the wolf's, is used by coyotes for the same reasons.

Around our home in Paradise Valley, we are fortunate to hear coyotes singing year-round, but they are most vocal from September through winter. Often during an October dusk one animal will begin with a series of short yips that blend into a lonely howl. Another usually answers, then they are joined by other kin chiming in from other directions. Most of the time they do not even pause when I add an extra voice to their chorus.

Scientists who have studied coyotes do not fully understand howling. Sometimes a chorus sounds like commiseration or communion with lost canid souls, while other times it is fairly harmonious and penetrating, maybe a declaration of territorial ownership. Once, when hiking up Deep Creek close to home, I heard a single coyote barking more and more insistently the farther upstream I moved. When eventually I stumbled upon an active den in the streambank, I realized that all along the barking coyote had been warning of my approach. A single coyote yipping or bark-howling might also be a challenge to other unfamiliar coyotes to keep their distance. Although I cannot altogether dispel the

Opposite above: Before the coyotes abandoned this elk carcass, also a victim of a harsh winter, they had recycled every last ounce of meat and some of the bone. When little edible matter remains, charity is forgotten and only the strongest, most dominant coyote is left to feed.

Opposite below: Despite the frozen landscape of winter, either by instinct or prior passage, coyotes know the easiest routes to travel, where the snow pack is hardest and deep drifts can be avoided.

notion that coyotes howling in a group are just enjoying themselves; they do not just bay at the moon as is often believed.

On one occasion, first through binoculars and later through a long telephoto lens, I watched a coyote howling beside the carcass of a partially eaten deer. Exactly why, it is impossible to say, but during the next hour or so, until dusk, no other coyotes answered or arrived to share the meal. It seems clear that coyotes do not howl to advertise a food source to others (see pages 64–65).

Like most of the world's wild dogs, coyotes are territorial. A mated pair of adults will leave their territory, their hunting range, only under duress, almost always when the local food supply falls short. Coyotes may also leave a familiar territory in search of a new mate. Young coyotes must eventually leave the territory of their birth to find and settle in a new area of their own, which may entail a lot of risky wandering and invading of other already established territories.

Above: Like wolves, coyotes often hunt beside waterways, especially in summer. Although rodents make up most of their diet, they do not pass up any frogs, salamanders, snakes, fish, or water birds they may find here. They also dine on eggs found in waterfowl nests.

Coyote territories average much smaller than those of gray wolves. In suitable areas well stocked with prey, one family may range over forty or fifty square miles. Poorer hunting territories may be twice that size. However, hunting areas in sanctuaries such as Yellowstone Park are not always exclusive. When severe winters kill many large animals on their wintering grounds, the carrion soon draws coyotes from far away. Brief fights may occur with the arrival of newcomers. Interlopers are sometimes tolerated at the carcass, though never near immediate denning areas within established territories.

Not many mammals, and very few carnivores, are able to live well on a diet as varied as that of the super dog. Biologists have analyzed coyote stomach contents in various parts of North America and one man, Charles Sperry, has examined over eight thousand. The results of all the studies are pretty much the same. Coyotes depend on smaller mammals, especially rodents, for half of all their bulk and nutrition. Rabbits, hares, gophers, ground squirrels, and especially mice are what a coyote is most likely to encounter during a typically meandering, haphazard hunting trip across its territory. But these hunters will also eat any birds, insects, reptiles, amphibians, or even fish they can catch. All kinds of vegetable matter, including some forbs and

especially fruit, are consumed, too. I have watched coyotes catch grasshoppers during August, when the insects swarmed in our fields; in an Arizona study, one coyote's stomach contained five hundred grasshoppers. Rattlesnakes, meadowlarks, frogs, blackbirds, fallen apples, and persimmons are all fair game. So are large mammals, wild and domestic, depending on the season and the locality. But the coyote's reputation as a predator of big game and livestock is greatly exaggerated. Much of both found in coyote stomachs come from carrion.

Venison appears in large quantities in some coyote stomachs during fall and late winter, which is during and after the annual hunting seasons when deer and elk escape from hunters crippled, or when the large animals, at the end of a long winter, are perishing from starvation. Coyotes certainly will attack deer that are in a weakened condition and unable to run. They also make good use of any road kills, from armadillos to opossums to porcupines.

Coyotes may capture deer fawns when they happen upon one that is very young and unable to escape, as well as domestic calves. Nowadays more and more stockmen seem willing to write off occasional stock losses because the coyote is a definite asset as a killer of rabbits and rodents that eat grass that would otherwise feed their animals. It is a rare

sheepman, however, who regards any coyote as anything but his worst enemy and a criminal.

Most of the time, unlike wolves, coyotes are lone hunters. Almost everything coyotes eat can be subdued or caught by a single animal. They also employ hunting tactics that suggest a measure of intelligence. For example, pairs of coyotes have been seen crisscrossing sagebrush flats, never overlapping paths, in areas where antelope mothers are known to drop fawns in springtime. More than once observers have seen this tactic pay off. White-tailed deer and elk mothers, as well as female antelope, use a "hider strategy" to protect their young. Following the birth, the females eat not only the natal membranes, but also the earth beneath, which contains birth fluids, in order to eliminate the scent a predator might detect. Calves or fawns are then left behind, hidden for long periods between nursings, while the mother is away feeding and attracting any attention to herself, and away from her young. Coyotes, especially packs of them, will always locate a small percentage of these

Above: Occasionally, when traveling in winter a coyote will flush a mouse from its nest under the snow. When that happens, it quickly has a welcome, though small meal. Thanks to its keen senses, coyotes are able to locate mice under the snow and pounce on them before they actually see the prey.

young before they are old enough to outrun the hunters, but a mother's actions ensure that many will survive. One morning in eastern Wyoming, for example, Peggy and I watched a very determined antelope mother drive a pair of coyotes away from a fawn that was still unsteady afoot.

Whether hunting alone or with others, the super dog owes its success to a combination of stamina and the most acute sensory equipment. A coyote can scan a landscape and detect more details than most other animals or any human. For instance, it can spot a mouse moving in grass beyond the point where the mouse is visible to people. The song dog's ears, larger for its size than a wolf's, gather faint sounds that pinpoint an unseen prey's exact position. Time and again in Yellowstone Park, where the coyotes pay little attention to tourists who watch them hunting, we have seen traveling individuals suddenly pause, pounce, and emerge from tall grass with a mouse or meadow vole. No doubt a keen sense of smell also enables a coyote to locate a meal it cannot see: for example, beneath a blanket of snow.

The wild cats and other carnivores depend on a combination of claws and teeth for killing prey, like rabbits and other larger creatures, but coyotes rely on sharp, enamel-capped teeth alone. Prey is immobilized when it is grasped by the throat and suffocated. In fact, a coyote kill can always be identified by tooth punctures around the throat.

Small mammals and birds may be swallowed whole. Much predation to both deer and domestic sheep by free-roaming packs of domestic dogs has been blamed on coyotes, but the trademark mangled flanks and hindquarters show that the blame is wrongly placed.

On a few occasions we have watched coyotes chasing seemingly healthy adult deer and elk fawns, but never successfully. Although coyotes may be fast enough afoot to catch or keep up with them, bringing down a tenacious deer with its sharp, kicking hooves, is another matter.

I confess the greatest admiration, even affection and partiality, for this medium-sized wild canid. In some ways it is like a smart supermarket shopper always looking for the best bargains of the day. A neighbor of mine could bring a certain coyote running from afar just by shaking his tree full of ripening apples. But the wary animal would not come near enough to collect the fallen fruit unless my friend remained out of sight and indoors. Only then would the coyote carry away as many apples as it could, as quickly as possible, to some hidden cache. (Caching food for later use is a species trait.)

Every coyote that reaches adulthood lives a life on the defensive. You can sense it in the furtive yellow eyes that always seem to be considering all the options. You can see it in the way coyotes avoid humans and human "territories," at least during daylight. Any observer will find a lot of coyote tracks and signs before ever seeing the coyote. Maybe more than any other wild creature, this one possesses an uncanny sensitivity to any threat to its own welfare.

Life begins for a coyote in a well-hidden, usually underground den in a litter of from two to twelve siblings. Five or six is the average, though there is one record litter of seventeen pups.

The parents, mated for life, begin or renew a courtship when snow still covers much of their range. Mating takes place between late January and early March. Gestation lasts about two months.

Rather than leaving for a bachelor life, fathers take part in raising pups by hunting to supply the family with food. Young from litters born one or two years earlier may also help feed the family and take turns patrolling the den site. When the parents have helpers on hand, pup survival rates (defined as the age at which pups reach full adult size—about nine months) seem to improve. Some litters scatter by early autumn, others remain relatively intact through the winter.

A few young remain somewhere within their natal territory, perhaps for security, occasionally joining the family on hunts. Others move away—the riskier choice. Young animals comprise most of the 80 percent mortality rate attributed to human trapping, shooting, poisoning, and other control schemes. Parasites, canine distemper, and hepatitis also take a toll, as does predation. In Yellowstone Park a young female that had been tagged was killed

Opposite above: Ground squirrels exist everywhere in the original western range of the coyote. In spring and summer these rodents and their offspring can sustain a growing coyote family occupying the same territory. Younger ground squirrels are always easier to catch than adults, especially before the vegetation grows tall.

Opposite below: Coyotes hunt in family groups more in some areas than others. Although these are fully grown, they are seven-to-eight-month-old littermates not yet as skillful at hunting as they will soon become. Some or all of these will remain with their parents over the winter and may help care for and feed the next litter.

by a cougar near a carcass that belonged to the big cat. In the far north wolves prey on coyotes. The maximum known age of a wild coyote, tagged when a pup, was over twelve years, but the average age from birth might be only two or three years.

Once, on a hiking trip to photograph spring wildflowers in Wyoming's Grand Teton National Park, I located a coyote den that may have been the enlarged burrow of a ground squirrel. On a knoll, the site was surprisingly conspicuous, although difficult to approach, located not far from a chain of beaver ponds. It was only the third coyote den I had ever found. For three consecutive years the den was used for raising litters of pups; through a spotting scope I often watched from a distance.

During a lifetime of observing wildlife, few incidents ever matched the pleasant sight of the coyote mother suddenly appearing at the entrance to what seemed to be only a vacant hole in the ground. Quickly, six pups would tumble out and climb all

Opposite: This young coyote has found the nest of a Brewer's blackbird and appears uncertain, at least at first, what to do with it. A moment later, when the camera was empty of film, it gobbled the eggs and left the scene.

Above: This coyote must be well fed, as it plays, catlike, with a mouse caught in an open snow-covered field. Most mice are eaten immediately.

over the female in apparent joy. Once I saw the mother nursing the pups, standing up as coyotes commonly do. Another evening I saw her carrying one of the pups away, and after that no coyote was ever seen in the vicinity again.

It is well known that coyotes will move their offspring to an alternate site if they believe their den has been discovered, carrying or dragging the pups away one at a time in their mouths. One female, also in Wyoming, ferried five young to a second den two miles from the first in the course of a single night, traveling twenty miles altogether. All of the young survived the trip.

Surely the most interesting coyote incident I ever saw occurred early one spring in Yellowstone Park. Having seen two young grizzly bears walking toward us along the raised bank across the Snake River, we carefully approached from our side. The bears were then, and remained, unaware of our presence. They were ambling along apparently without a care, when suddenly, seemingly from nowhere, a coyote appeared, racing toward the bears, snarling and yipping, dancing on stiff legs. Taken by surprise, the bruins halted in their tracks, watching the coyote with apparent disbelief.

The smaller animal never paused, but dashed at the intruders, snapping her jaws all the while.

Thoroughly alarmed, one bear stood on its hind legs while the coyote continued to run at them, circle back a bit, then boldly approach once more. In a move psychologists might call transference, one bear slapped the other hard with a flying paw. Then both, thinking now only how to escape this mad creature, ran full tilt into the nearby lodgepole pines, never to return. Satisfied, the coyote seemed to take a deep breath, then slowly walked to the steep bank of the river, where now we saw the den she had dug just a few feet from the path the grizzlies had taken. The gritty little animal disappeared into the den, having sent packing in complete disarray perhaps one of the most fearsome animals on the continent.

With feats like this it is not surprising that the species as a whole has been spectacularly successful at surviving the twentieth century. Trying to eliminate or even to thin out numbers of this consummate omnivore has been like digging a hole in the ocean. But the same cannot be said of the coyote's closest relative, the red wolf, *Canis rufus*.

First, it is by no means agreed among taxonomists that the red wolf is a distinct species. Some recent genetic research that raises questions about what constitutes a species suggests that the red wolf might be a mutt—a cross between a gray wolf and a coyote. More than a century ago, the naturalist/painter John James Audubon thought it was simply a small gray subspecies. Even if that proves in time to be true, this mutt is still a most interesting wild dog, quite different in its habits from either the gray wolf or the coyote, although more like the coyote.

At this point, there still may be a few people alive in the United States who have heard the haunting melodies—the night howling—of both red and gray wolves, as well as of coyotes. They would probably place the red wolf's song between the other two in pitch, but closer to a coyote than a gray wolf. In shape and silhouette the red wolf most resembles a coyote and sometimes the two are indistinguishable. But, in fact, the red wolf is darker, more reddish in color, sometimes accentuated with black. At fifty pounds or more, an adult red wolf averages heavier than a full-grown coyote and lighter than a gray wolf. To maintain itself a red wolf requires a territory smaller than a gray, but larger than a coyote. However, the truth is that we know little about the red wolf's territory or the rest of its life history.

Red wolves were originally residents of the southeastern United States, where they were locally abundant. Early settlers in the Carolinas and Louisiana knew them well. Their original range extended from Florida northward to the Ohio River and westward in a wide band as far as central Texas. Nowhere in that entire area were they more than scapegoats for all the problems of pioneers trying to subdue a primeval land. Although far less a threat than floods, climate, sickness, or mosquitoes, the red wolves (like gray wolves and other wild dogs elsewhere) that did eat some chickens and livestock were blamed for everything. By about 1920, all the states east of the Mississippi River had probably been cleared of them.

Less suspicious of humans, reds were always a lot easier to trap and poison than coyotes. When the forests west of the Mississippi were felled, the land plowed, and predator control programs begun, the red wolf could no longer cope. Its ages-old society was destroyed, and when families stopped defending territories, coyotes filled the vacuum, either by replacing the red wolves or interbreeding with them. Only in southeastern Texas and southwestern Louisiana coastal swamps did a few red wolves survive in the wild, dying out completely by 1970. On a photo trip to Anahuac National Wildlife Refuge in 1968, it's possible that the two wild dogs I saw may have been pure red wolves, but that could be wishful thinking.

In the early 1970s, a program was launched to save red wolves, but many feared it may have been started too late. One project scientist estimated that only fifty reds, at most, were left. The aim of the program was to live-trap any wild dogs found in the Louisiana-Texas border area, and by X-raying skulls, to determine the ratio of brain volume to skull, and by conducting other tests, to learn if the captives were genuine reds, hybrids, or coyotes.

Altogether four hundred animals were trapped and examined. Some were determined to be pure reds and were retained in captive breeding centers. The rest were released where they had originally been trapped. But they soon vanished or interbred themselves out of existence. By about 1980, *Canis*

Opposite: Coyotes howl at any time and probably for different reasons, mostly for communicating within the family and declaring territory. However, most of the howling takes place between dusk and dawn and, depending on atmospheric pressure, can be heard from far away.
Following spread: This coyote was seen after finding and feeding on a deer carcass. The deer might have been the prey of a cougar, or it might have been injured in a rutting fight with another buck. No other coyote responded to the howling, which almost certainly was not an invitation to share the bounty.

rufus was extinct in the wild. The entire gene pool of this species, fourteen captives, was in custody at government research stations.

The behavior, breeding, gestation period, and family life of red wolves were probably very much like coyotes. Litter sizes ranged from three to a dozen, but pup mortality was judged to be high because many parasites, such as hookworm, thrive in the usually hot and humid areas they preferred. Young normally remained with their parents for a second year to form family groups. Fully grown eastern animals tended to be larger and darker in color than western ones. I once saw an almost all-black pelt that had been taken in Florida about a century ago.

What has happened since 1980 has often been encouraging. In a game of musical mates, the fourteen captives have been transferred from one facility to another for breeding to promote as much genetic diversity as possible. The number alive reached two hundred in 1992. But raising captives and merely opening cage doors will not successfully reintroduce a carnivorous species into the wild. The animals have to be acclimated gradually to living wild on wild prey. Suitable places to release them, with no wild coyotes (with whom they would interbreed) had to be found.

Bull Island, South Carolina, seemed an ideal place. However, the first captives, two pairs, released at Bull Island in 1985 did not fare well; some died of infection and some disappeared. But valuable lessons in handling and acclimatization were learned. Local farmer opposition prevented a second release at Land Between the Lakes, Kentucky, and near a plutonium and tritium production plant along the Savannah River in South Carolina. But the Alligator River National Wildlife Refuge, also in South Carolina, seemed perfect.

A peninsula surrounded by the Alligator River and by Albemarle, Croatan, and Pamlico sounds, dank woodlands alternate there with swamps and marshlands in total solitude. It contains a good wildlife population, including many species on which red wolves could prey: rabbits, opossums, muskrats, reptiles, birds, and wild turkeys. It is also the northernmost habitat in America of alligators and contains a few black bears, both of which might be red wolf competitors. Best of all, coyotes had not colonized the Alligator River refuge.

The first pair of captive-bred wolves was released at the Alligator refuge in 1987, and additional releases were made thereafter. Five years later, U.S. Fish & Wildlife Service biologists estimated that sixteen healthy reds were roaming free. Encouraged by their success, they were already thinking about trapping surplus wolves and transferring them to other suitable sites.

More than eighty-six years after they were last observed, probably over the barrel of a rifle, red wolves were seen again in another old haunt—Great Smoky Mountains National Park, Tennessee, where two pair have been freed with surgically implanted radio transmitters. At the time this book was written in 1993, they were still living. Park officials believe the park might be able to support fifty to seventy-five of the native wild dogs.

Only time will tell if red wolves become the first wild dogs or the first wild carnivores to be safely reestablished after being declared extinct. The odds seem favorable. Habitats in their historic range included forests, both hardwood and deciduous, coastal plains, and wetlands, much of which is less than ideal for coyotes. Red wolves were even known to scavenge along the Gulf of Mexico beaches. Among the other few facts we know about them is that they are more likely to cooperate with others of their species when hunting than coyotes are. What few, credible early accounts survive reveal that red wolves hunted turkeys and especially white-tailed deer. Naturalist Mark Catesby wrote in 1743 that red wolves "go in droves by night and hunt deer like hounds with dismal yelling cries."

How true to life Catesby's account was will never be known, but most would agree that it would be a thrilling sound to hear again. Saving the red wolf means making a commitment to saving its environment and ours for the future.

■

Opposite: In winter the coyote moves ghostlike through northern woods and is far more likely to be heard than seen. During this season its pelt is heavy and sleek.

Following spread: All across America, coyotes have adapted well to agricultural areas, or at least to the fringes of farms where ring-necked pheasants may supplement a diet of small mammals. Coyotes may concentrate on pheasants during the hunting season, when birds are often crippled by shooters and unable to fly.

Opposite: Perhaps from unremitting persecution, coyotes always seem to be living on the edge—on the defensive. Every adult is on full-time alert, watching for both prey and natural enemies. Human beings are their biggest threat.

Above: Hunting along the edge of a northern woodland, a coyote finds and flushes a snowshoe hare from its form, as hare's dens are known. Despite the hare's speed, the coyote catches it after a short chase. The coyote gulped down most of it on the spot and carried away the forequarters.

Above: Coyote pups remain very close to the natal den for a few months after they are born blind and helpless. A den may be beneath a deadfall or undercut bank or in a burrow abandoned by a woodchuck or ground squirrel.

Opposite page: From three to five months, the more precocious coyote young explore farther and farther from the den. Pups in some litters seem to play and play-fight (to determine ranking) more than others. If the den is discovered or threatened, the female will move young to an alternate den.

Right: This coyote moved six pups from a den just out of sight in the background to a site probably a mile away.

Opposite: Once nearly full grown, a young coyote is an agile, quick traveler in the woods. It may not yet be the consummate hunter, but little escapes its notice. If it survives its first full year, each coyote is a genuine super dog.

Above: The red wolf, which some scientists believe is a mutt or a coyote-wolf cross, is somewhere between the two and resembles both. It is larger and slightly more reddish than the coyote, especially those from the north, and it is not as likely to be a solitary hunter. Red wolves have not survived the advance of civilization nearly as well as the super dog. Once thought extinct, today a small number again lives in the wild, thanks to long-term programs of reestablishment into a few former ranges. Only time will tell if these programs succeed.

Opposite: A coyote yawns in the afternoon sun, exposing a full set of razor-sharp teeth.

Above: With its keen senses of sight, smell, and hearing, the coyote is vastly more adaptable and a better survivor than all other species of wild dog.

Above: This animal is a red wolf-coyote hybrid captured in Louisiana. However this positive identification was possible only through X-rays and other laboratory tests. Seen in the wild, it passes easily for either a coyote or a red wolf.

Opposite: Winter is a tough test for every coyote in the northern limits of its range. Without the bonanza of winter-killed big game, an animal must travel far over snowy landscapes, beneath which many small animals hibernate, in order to find enough nutrition to survive.

Right, below and bottom: Some time ago coyotes learned they could catch more ground squirrels when hunting with—actually following—badgers into ground squirrel colonies than they could when hunting alone. When the pair first approach, the nervous, watchful squirrels disappear into their burrows underground, where the badger locates them through scent and sound. When the digging badger gets too close, the squirrels dart out through other exits, where the coyote stands waiting. Both hunters benefit from this partnership.

Many wildlife species serve as wild dog prey. Both coyotes and red wolves will catch wild turkeys (above left), especially before chicks are able to fly each spring. The Uinta ground squirrel (below), here chirping a warning, is fair game for Wyoming coyotes. Adult ring-necked pheasants (above) are most likely to be caught in fall and winter. Canadian geese (left) nesting along lakeshores are very vulnerable, and in some places coyotes will often specialize in them.

Right: Black bears also share territory with coyotes. The desiccated elk carcass might have been picked clean earlier by coyotes or it might have been stolen from them by the bruin.

Below right: The range of the American bobcat overlaps that of the coyote, red wolf, and all native foxes except the Arctic fox. Everywhere it is a competitor of varying degree for some available prey. Bobcats might also kill coyote pups caught away from their den.

Below: Remains of prairie rattlesnakes have often been found in the stomachs of coyotes. Since snakes also eat rodents, they compete with wild dogs for food.

Above left: Raccoons are common competitors in coyote country, particularly in the eastern and southern regions.

Left: The Florida panther was once and could again be a direct competitor with red wolves. Both carnivores hunt deer, wild turkeys, wild hogs, and other southern creatures.

Above: Young pronghorn antelope on the western plains are natural prey for coyotes, which deliberately hunt lambs during lambing season. But a healthy, full-grown antelope can easily outrun a coyote or drive it away from a threatened fawn.

FOXES

Nine species of the genus *Vulpes*, the foxes, together occupy almost every region of the world's northern hemisphere, as well as much of Africa. One species or another thrives in every type of terrain and at all but the highest altitudes. European settlers brought foxes for pest control to Australia, where they are now well established. Some of the vulpine species are desert inhabitants while others prefer humid forests, tundra, or high plains. But none have adapted to so many environments or become more widely distributed throughout the world today than *Vulpes vulpes*, the red or true fox. This is the flamboyant and cunning canid of myth and folklore that comes to mind when we think of foxes. In the sixteenth century, Italian Prince Machiavelli observed that "to survive in this world, a man must learn to play like a fox." Hence the word "Machiavellian," meaning sly or shifty behavior. In the biblical Song of Solomon, reds were "the little foxes that spoil the vines."

If any wild dog matches the coyote in its ability to cope with civilization, it is this fox. Although it has been hunted incessantly for sport and trapped for its fine, pumpkin-colored pelt, it continues to thrive. But the red fox is also a mystery. Few farmers think of foxes as friends, although they should. What we

Left: A female red fox returns cautiously to her den, but does not enter. This den has another entrance facing a different direction in case of danger.

tend to regard as a familiar animal is too seldom seen in the wild and is not really familiar at all. One admirer, the pioneer conservationist Aldo Leopold, once commented that "rowdy red the fox seems to sneer at man."

I was a young boy in Ohio when I first listened to a story I have heard many times since. It is true that sometimes in summer foxes become infested with fleas that make their lives uncomfortable. To get rid of the irritants, according to the yarn, a fox will swim out into a lake or pond with a twig in its mouth until only the tip of its nose is visible above the surface. Like rats leaving a doomed ship, the fleas are said to escape onto the twig, which the fox leaves adrift, returning to land completely free of the unwanted pests. Even if this does not actually happen, the story says much about the real or supposed intellect of the species.

The red fox stands only a foot or slightly more at the shoulder, weighs between eight and ten pounds fully grown, and has a bushy tail longer than its height, which streams straight out behind it when it runs. Males are only slightly larger than females. Thick and silky fur makes coat and tail seem much larger than they really are. The red fox shares one very distinctive feature, its eyes, with other members of its genus. The pupil forms an ellipsis or a vertical slit when exposed to bright light. In wolves and coyotes the pupil also becomes smaller, but round in

Right: Three of the pups in this den (same as on page 84) would make occasional forays from underground, but remained in the immediate area. Here, they are now seven to eight weeks old. These pups did not tumble and play-fight as much as in some other litters.

shape. Although probably more active during daylight hours, reds are well equipped for night hunting.

Few humans ever approach near enough to notice, but all red foxes emit a strong odor from oversized (compared to other wild dogs) scent glands located around the anus, on top of the base of the tail, and on the pads of the feet. So strong is the odor that at times it can betray the presence or the den of a red fox to a very skilled and experienced woodsman. The more frightened or excited the animal becomes, the stronger the scent and thus the easier it is for fox hounds or wild predators to follow its trail—a distinct disadvantage. But the scent also sends a strong signal of its presence to all other red foxes, so unwanted confrontations are avoided.

Not all red foxes are really red, although a vivid reddish back with a white belly is the most common color phase, especially in southern parts of the range. There are three color phases or types—red, cross, and black or silver—and each has several variations. Individuals of the red phase range from pale yellow or tan to bright orange, and they may have gray or black rather than white bellies. Some are nearly black or have black shading on the legs, along the spine, or over the shoulder.

The only black-phase red fox I have ever seen was in central Alaska. It was completely coal-colored, relieved only by a white tip on its tail. Black phases can also appear brownish, slate, blue, or silver, the last because of white or gray guardhairs growing out of darker underfur. Cross phase foxes are reddish yellow to brown or brindled with a dark cross over the shoulders. Crosses make up from a fifth to a fourth of all red foxes. At birth all color phases are a pale gray.

Every red fox molts each spring. The molt progresses from shoulders to rump as long guardhairs grow brittle, lose their luster, and fall out. Next, clumps of underfur drop away, and for a month or so the foxes seem afflicted with a severe case of mange. One morning at low tide along the Alaskan coast, we watched a red fox that was almost hairless beachcombing for whatever marine creatures were exposed at water's edge. Its hairlessness suggested it was diseased, but its quick, darting movements revealed a healthy animal whose appearance would greatly improve before the end of summer. When the first snow falls, there are few animals more handsome than a northern red fox with its long and luxuriant coat.

Above: Adult red foxes spend long periods during daylight asleep or half-asleep, curled up with their tails covering their faces, even in rain or snowstorms. They often choose resting places that allow them to spot danger approaching from any direction.

Watching red foxes for over forty years has provided more pleasure and more surprises than it is possible for me to recount. Among the most indelible occurred on a warm July evening in Grand Teton National Park when I sat hidden in deep forest overlooking a meadow of mountain wildflowers. Before dusk a red fox appeared, and in the last rays of a low sun raced back and forth at top speed, hunting, sneaking, and pouncing on mice. It caught some, failed to capture many more, and altogether gave an athletic performance of Olympian quality that was still in progress when the meadow finally faded into deep-blue shadow (see page 92–93).

That evening also illustrated how and why the red fox has evolved into a mostly solitary hunter. When emerging above ground to feed, its prey, often mice, are naturally nervous and quick of movement. To capture them the fox must be even more swift. A single fox has a better chance than two or more at surprising prey that needs only a split second to disappear into a burrow or dash into a tree. It is interesting to note that a fox's hearing is most sensitive to low frequencies, such as rodents moving in vegetation or gnawing on seeds and twigs, than to sounds in the upper range. In fact, a hunting fox, by hearing alone, can locate its prey almost exactly. By contrast, the hearing of most other mammals, including humans, is better attuned to higher notes, such as the distress calls of its young and of other creatures.

Biologists estimate that a healthy red fox can travel through dense brush at speeds up to thirty miles per hour, seeming to glide over deadfalls or duck under them with equal ease. That is fast enough to capture most of the sixty-three species of small mammals, birds, and insects found in its diet, according to one Missouri study. However, just three staples—cottontail rabbits, meadow voles, and insects—made up two-thirds of that total. A snowshoe hare or jackrabbit is as large a prey as a red fox can handle. Young birds, like quail, pheasants, and grouse are caught and eaten each spring.

In late summer and fall, especially during years of abundance, foxes eat quantities of both wild and cultivated fruits and berries. Red foxes have never endeared themselves to farmers whose melon fields they invade. An orchard where ripened apples or

pears have fallen to the ground is a good place to watch at daybreak and dusk for red foxes, as well as for coyotes and gray foxes.

Unless it is a female tending to pups around a den or a couple during courtship, a red fox is either at total rest or engaged in a lifelong search for food. Total rest means curling up in a ball, bushy tail covering the eyes, in a spot where the sleeper can fitfully scan the surrounding landscape and make an escape if need be (see photo on page 87). The fox will curl up that way whether in balmy June or brutal January, when a snowfall may completely cover it. Once when hunting pheasants during a snowstorm years ago, a sleeping and greatly startled fox exploded from the white ground almost at my feet. It isn't often that any red fox is taken so completely by surprise. Once flushed, the startled fox was out of sight in seconds.

When not sleeping, foxes hunt, which means traveling back and forth across their territories, at first seemingly at random. Territory size depends on the abundance of prey within it. But foxes will follow game trails or any paths of least resistance, often using man-made thoroughfares like roads, irrigation ditches, and hiking trails, making frequent detours to check on smells and other sensor-derived information. They try to capture and eat whatever

prey they come across. Anything that cannot be eaten on the spot is cached. Based on my own experiences during the 1950s in agricultural central Ohio, red foxes hunted in pairs or at least on parallel paths, especially in winter, more often than biologists report now. I think they are also much less vocal than the larger wild dogs.

Reds have a variety of calls that range from yapping, barking, growling, and howling to something like screaming. Some sounds serve to keep mates in touch, while others designate territories and warn away interlopers. However, scent from urinating, defecating, or glandular secretions seems much more important than sound in marking territories. By far the noisiest foxes I ever heard were the half-grown pups in a Montana den. To punctuate bouts of play-fighting, which at times became almost vicious, the siblings would scream at one another. It is surprising that these penetrating sounds, often repeated, did

Above: This den of young red foxes was beneath an old stone barn on an abandoned farm. The pups were so shy they almost never appeared during daylight. The den was probably an old groundhog burrow.

Right: This red fox had captured a gray or Canada jay, which it carried away either to a cache or a den of young.

not betray the den location to coyotes, black bears, or other predators that roamed the vicinity. I believe all five pups survived to adulthood.

Biologists who have studied both wild cats and canids believe red foxes are the most catlike of the wild dogs. They do share numerous physical features and habits. Reds, as well as some other fox species, have long whiskers on both the muzzle and carpal joints or wrists that work as tactile organs. The wrist whiskers probably help guide the fox when stalking and the muzzle whiskers help the fox aim its lethal bites in exactly the right direction.

Red foxes also have the long, thin canine teeth found in cats. Unlike many other predators that must shake their prey vigorously, foxes and cats kill just by puncturing deeper with their canines. New layers of enamel are added every year to a red fox's teeth to compensate for daily wear and tear. Researchers can determine the animal's age by counting the teeth's cross-section growth rings.

Even the paws of a red fox are catlike. The claws on the front feet pull back just enough to be considered semiretractile. The pads are small and the lower foot is covered with hair, a combination that retains heat in cold weather and renders the feet more sensitive to touch, consequently allowing for a stealthy, quiet approach.

❖

The red fox has two close relatives in North America: *Vulpes macrotis*, the kit fox, and *Vulpes velox*, the swift fox. Great differences exist among taxonomists about whether these are really separate species or simply two subspecies. They are similar in appearance, but since they occupy different kinds of habitat, I will regard them as distinct species.

Originally, the swift fox was a native of the Great Plains. Early pioneers traveling west found them fairly common from the Texas Panhandle north to Alberta and Saskatchewan. They were nowhere as wary as gray wolves or, especially, coyotes. Weighing only four to five pounds when fully grown, half the weight of a red fox, swift foxes were easy to catch in steel traps. Nevertheless, they managed to survive fairly well until the late 1940s, when western ranchers began to demand increased predator control, and subsequently a new lethal menace, Compound 1080, was introduced.

The chemical 1080 was an odorless and, as far as anyone knew, tasteless, fine-grained, water-soluble, white powder. Without a smell or taste that would warn an animal away from bait laced with 1080, it was regarded as the perfect predator poison. Untold tons of this deadly substance, for which there is no antidote, were "applied" by government agents all across the Great Plains for more than a decade, mostly to kill coyotes. It is important to describe how it was done and how it worked.

In open range country—swift fox country—a horse, sick cow, or other bait animal would be killed and cut into a dozen pieces. A water solution of 1080 was injected into the still-warm meat with a long-needled "brine gun" that forced the poison liberally into the flesh. After the meat chunks stiffened for a day or two to seal the poison inside, the pieces were scattered wherever coyotes were found or suspected.

There is no way we will ever know the wildlife toll taken by 1080 bait during almost a quarter century of use, but the despicable practice killed indiscriminately and without conscience. One or two bites sealed any creature's fate, whether magpie or golden eagle, badger or black-footed ferret, cougar, coyote, or swift fox. And any scavenger that ate the poisoned victim was killed by the deadly compound as well.

The poison did not produce a quick, painless death. With its nervous system attacked, a swift fox would end up on its back wildly "running" in agony before finally dying. Under intense pressure from environmentalists in 1972, President Richard Nixon finally banned the use of 1080, but the ban seemed to have come too late to save the swift fox. They appeared to have gone the way of passenger pigeons and other vanished species. But not quite.

Suddenly, in the mid-eighties, fur trappers in eastern Wyoming began to find swift foxes in their sets after an absence of two decades. The species also seemed to return from the dead elsewhere. Both private and state conservation groups took a renewed interest in the species, and live-trapped surplus animals were taken from Wyoming and released into other parts of their original range. Although by no means abundant anywhere yet, today swift foxes are among the living. But because the buff-colored canid with a dark spot on each side of its snout is not valuable as either a game or fur-bearing animal, we have never bothered to learn much about its life history.

One thing I do know, from infrequent sightings, is that the swift is well named. It is an agile hunter of small prairie mammals and birds. Ironically, however, the adults may spend more time underground, as when resting, than any other North American wild dog. Several observers have reported that at

least some swift foxes will crouch motionless, blending into the ground to escape detection, rather than to run away, as do other wild dogs.

In southern Alberta, litters of four to seven pups are whelped (born) some time in March and raised and fed pretty much like pups of other fox species. Some adults dig their own home dens, but most seem just to enlarge prairie dog or ground squirrel burrows. A swift fox may also dig at least one other entrance in addition to the main den opening. One den in Canada was discovered with eight entrances.

Our knowledge of the kit fox is almost as limited as that of the swift fox. The kit fox is paler in color, has slightly larger ears for its size, and tends to carry food to a den or hiding place before eating it. A dweller of much drier habitat, the kit fox, like most other desert animals, is nocturnal for most of the year because a large part of its prey is also inactive until darkness descends. Even with modern technology, nocturnal species are more difficult to track and study than diurnal species. As a result there are great gaps in our knowledge of this smallest native dog, especially since it has no commercial value.

Naturalist Victor Cahalane in his *Mammals of North America* was the first to suggest that kit foxes are the fastest hunters in a short chase, giving two good reasons for that view. First, speed is vital to catching enough to eat. But even more important is

their apparent ability to escape from numerous potential enemies: cougars, coyotes, badgers, bobcats, eagles, larger hawks, and great horned owls.

A resident of the southwestern United States and northern Mexico, the kit fox either is not numerous anywhere or is so secretive it is seldom seen. Much of its best habitat, especially in southern California, has been claimed by ever-expanding suburbs, factories, and shopping malls. If kit foxes are to survive permanently in this greatly altered environment, they will have to make the same drastic adaptation to city life as the coyote.

❖

During my youth, I spent a lot of time roaming the woods of southern Ohio. While raccoon hunting one cold February night, our pack of hounds treed game after an hour-long chase through blackberry briers and rugged hill country. Arriving at the scene,

Above: Red fox adults, both shedding their winter pelage, romp and play near their Alaskan den, which is hidden in the background. The pair continued the play for a long time in a soft drizzle.

Following spread: A young red fox romps across a Rocky Mountain meadow, trying unsuccessfully to catch mice or ground squirrels. Even young foxes are extremely quick and lithe in all their movements.

I searched the bare branches in the crown of a spreading oak tree with the beam of my flashlight. What I found on a branch about ten feet above me was not a 'coon at all, but a fox. It was, in fact, my first gray fox encounter. Until then all the foxes I had seen were reds.

In general appearance the two are similar and in silhouette alone they are almost impossible to tell apart, with their long pointed noses and bushy tails. But the closer the inspection the more apparent the differences became. A gray fox's legs are shorter as are its tail and muzzle. Its coat is coarser than a red fox and grizzled or salt-and-pepper on the back and belly. The sides of the face, ears, legs, and flanks are lighter, reddish, or rust colored. There is a black tip on the tail and usually, a black stripe extends all the way down the spine. Altogether, the gray fox, *Urocyon cinereoargenteus*, is a striking animal the color of autumn, whether it is running across a sunlit pasture or looking down from an old oak tree.

The range of the gray fox, which covers all of the United States except the northwestern quarter as well as northern Mexico and Baja California (where it is called *chacolillo*), overlaps with the range of all other North American foxes, except the Arctic fox. In habits, habitat, hunting, and almost every other characteristic, the gray fox is a composite of the others, but with a few notable differences. Whereas a red fox will undertake a long, cross-country run, a trait that endeared it to the red coat and foxhound hunting society, grays retreat into underground dens or the densest brush or quickly scale trees.

In trees, not only do they find refuge, but unlike all other wild dogs, gray foxes are able to forage in them as well. This is done by gripping a trunk (best with a rough bark) with its forepaws, then gradually pushing itself higher with the long claws on its rear feet. The animal is comfortable enough in some trees to be able to jump or climb from limb to limb when hunting birds, especially small bird nests that contain eggs or hatchlings. Most of the time grays back down from trees the same way they climb up, but I saw at least one jump down from a height of about five feet.

Whereas the red fox prefers the edge of a habitat, such as between forest and field or farm and wetland, the gray is more a woodland fox, especially at home in the colorful canyon country of Utah and

Left above: A young red fox engages a littermate in play-fighting that almost seems vicious. Their noisy scuffling is punctuated with loud screams.

Left: One red fox pup finally captures a ground squirrel and shows no intention whatever of sharing it with littermates.

New Mexico. One morning, on a dawn hike in Bryce Canyon National Park, I had the feeling I was being followed. I stopped at a sharp bend in the trail to look around. Not far above, almost hidden on a ledge in the red sandstone canyon wall, a gray fox watched me intently for several minutes before disappearing.

Gray foxes mate at a year old, sometime between late January and March. Gestation is about two months, and litters run from two to seven black pups, weighing about three ounces each, helpless and with their eyes closed. Males remain with females and support them by delivering food for about six weeks or until the young are weaned. Pups remain with the parents for a few months after weaning, longer if prey is scarce. Gray foxes have been reported to spend an entire winter in family groups. They have been clocked running at 28 miles per hour for short distances and appear to be short-winded.

In many areas the gray, called the cat fox in parts of the Southeast, spends daylight hours in a den underground, in a hollow log or tree, or some other secure, dark refuge. Nights are devoted to hunting in territories that are smaller than those of red foxes. Grays will eat at least as many types of creatures and fruits as other foxes. They can't resist trees full of ripening persimmons, wild grapes, wild black cherries, or apples. In one study in the Southwest, more than half of all gray fox stomachs contained spiders, centipedes, or scorpions, the latter complete with stingers and poison glands. In Ohio, a gray fox was observed eating Halloween pumpkins placed by farm children beside a rural mailbox.

It appears that gray foxes are not very long-lived. One Georgia study discovered that fewer than 10 percent of the animals in the area were two years old or older. Parasites and disease were believed responsible. In a New York study, only one adult over two could be found.

❖

If one species of fox differs most from the others, it is *Alopex lagopus*, the white or Arctic fox. This northernmost wild dog roams the lonely, barren fringe at the top of North America, in Greenland, and across northernmost Eurasia, from treeline to well beyond the polar ice pack. No wild dog in the world lives in a harsher environment, or is better equipped to do so. Its fur rates high among the finest natural insulators known, which means that, unfor-

tunately, the pelts score equally high with fur trappers and commercial furriers.

A healthy Arctic fox's coat maintains warmth so well that winter temperatures can plunge to –20° or –25°F before the animal's metabolic rate begins to increase to compensate for lost body heat. Thick hair even grows over its pads and claws, keeping the feet warm on ice or in powder snow and providing traction when needed. To retain heat, the ears of the Arctic fox are shorter and more rounded than other fox species. We know that white foxes can survive, even remain active, when the temperature drops as low as –60°F.

These adaptations to a terribly cold environment have important advantages. Rather than having to increase its caloric intake—to find and catch more prey—as other mammals would have to do, this fox can continue its travels over vast distances on no more food than it might need in summer. That explains its ability to survive in the Arctic, where food varies from scarce to unavailable throughout the long winter.

Above: An Artic fox approaches the edge of a stream in search of food.

Not all Arctic foxes are white, even in winter. All of those living on Alaska's Pribilof Islands, St. George and St. Paul, are of a blue phase. In summer the short hair of both white and blue phases is tawny to brown on the back and yellowish underneath. In various parts of their range there are intermediates between blue and white adults. Pups are grayish or white and gray or tan at birth.

During brief summertimes, Arctic foxes usually live the good life, especially during those years when brown, collared, or bog lemmings are numerous. Populations of these three to five-inch vole-like mammals fluctuate greatly from high to very low in four-year cycles. Fox populations move up and down accordingly. The foxes usually reach their peak numbers one or two years after the lemming population peaks.

In some areas of the Arctic where there are great colonies of nesting seabirds along the ocean shores or where waterfowl and shorebirds nest on tundra inland, foxes naturally take as much advantage as possible of the annual spring bounty. Mostly, they eat eggs or carry away nestlings. I have had my share of interesting encounters with Arctic foxes and most of them were near seabird rookeries.

One morning Peggy and I planned to photograph the murres, kittiwakes, and puffins nesting on

the nearly vertical cliff faces of St. Paul Island in the Bering Sea. To find the best location I would crawl on my stomach to the edge of the cliff and peer over while Peggy held onto my ankles. Usually, what I saw was a dizzying view of hundreds of black and white birds crowded on ledges (see photo on page 118, top), often in high winds, five hundred feet above a pounding gray ocean surf. But on one occasion, I looked down into the face of a startled blue fox only about five feet below me on a ledge only inches wide, with yellow egg yolk on its muzzle. To this day I cannot figure out how the fox managed to climb into that precarious position and out again.

A few days later, on nearby St. George Island, we located an Arctic fox den by watching an adult carrying the carcasses of dead murres to a pile of driftwood logs washed high on a pebble beach. Through binoculars we saw three pups emerge from the flotsam and begin to pull the bird apart. Later, we erected a blind near that spot and were able to photograph the young foxes (see photo on page 114, bottom). At times they would venture very near to us, although the parent sat about 50 yards away, barking incessantly.

Foxes have learned to lurk around the bases of bird cliffs for nestlings that fall or are pushed off the cliffs. When they have more than they or their litters can eat, they cache all they can gather for the future. It is possible that these bird caches, freeze-dried, might even sustain them well into winter.

Arctic foxes are accomplished scavengers, too. During their widespread vagabonding they regularly come upon dead fish and marine mammals that have washed ashore. As with all wild dogs, this is an opportunity to gorge. They will also try to share scraps from the kills of wolves or polar bears, but that can be risky.

White foxes can breed when they are ten months old and, depending on how well the female has been nourished during the winter, will whelp anywhere from a single pup to as many as fourteen. Researchers once found an astonishing twenty-three embryos in an Arctic fox female. Even in the best of times, most pups do not reach breeding age. The pups weigh about two ounces at birth, and it is possible that they will be moved by the parents from the natal den to some other den nearer a food supply.

Friends in the Pribilofs tell me it is common to see females moving young from one place to another.

Above: Thanks to dense, insulating fur, the Artic fox can survive long, bitter, subzero cold spells on meager rations.

Right: Some Arctic foxes scavenge along the edges of ice packs; other follow polar bears all winter.

Opposite above: This male red fox is fully and beautifully furred by late summer, ready for the onset of cold weather. No members of the wild dog family are more striking, more handsome, when found in their natural environment than the red fox.

Opposite below: This female red fox has shed her winter coat. The long hairs are fading, becoming brittle, and falling away. She is very thin from nursing and caring for a litter.

Still, the same den sites, in rock piles or tundra eskers or beneath debris, are used year after year. There have been reports of more than one pair of adults raising pups in the same den at one time. There is also the possibility that these are the least monogamous of all the wild dogs, and polygamy may be common.

Wildlife photographers often become partial to species that are not shy, and the white fox fits this category. They soon become very tame around remote human outposts, camps, and villages where they are not shot or trapped. One day near Churchill, in far northern Manitoba, I saw a fox suddenly appear as if from nowhere. We were photographing one of the polar bears that spends the summer in the region until Hudson Bay freezes solid in the fall. Suddenly, a white fox entered my viewfinder and posed in the snow next to the bruin. The bear did not seem to be bothered by the fox (see photo on page 113, top).

For a part of their lives, at least, some Arctic foxes become marine rather than land mammals. For as long as six months each winter, a fox may wander over massive floating slabs of ice, never once touching solid ground. But these foxes are not moving aimlessly; one or a pair relentlessly follows a certain polar bear. When the bear kills a seal, it gorges, then sleeps nearby. The fox then moves in to fill its own stomach on the leftovers. If the bear is a successful hunter, the fox will have a bountiful winter and then return to land to bear pups in spring. If not, both bear and fox might starve.

Like the other wild dogs, white foxes are territorial on land. They may also be territorial on the ice pack, except that the territory, the area immediately surrounding the "adopted" polar bear wherever it chooses to go, changes daily, even hourly. Eskimos report that a fox or pair of foxes tracking a polar bear will drive other foxes away from their host.

Arctic foxes have their share of natural enemies. Just as the badger mentioned in the beginning of the book might someday dig out the pups of its coyote hunting companion and eat them, so might the polar bear dig out a den of fox pups. Wolves, wolverines, red foxes (where their ranges overlap), rough-legged hawks, gyrfalcons, and snowy owls are also potential natural enemies.

No one knows how many Arctic foxes exist today, but probably the remote white wilderness in which most live is sufficient protection, and we can assume the species continues to thrive. The fact that the fur farm industry in northern Europe has reduced the pressure for trapping wild animals also helps to protect the Arctic Fox.

Although *Alopex lagopus* is a difficult creature for anyone to see without undertaking a long trip to a remote part of North America, it is surely among the most attractive and endearing creatures on the face of the earth.

■

Above: Red foxes will follow game trails, country lanes, cowpaths, even roads—the paths of least resistance—when they are hunting. This adult was observed using the same fallen yellow birch as a bridge, over and over, to cross a cold mountain stream.

Right: A heavily shedding red fox combs a beach in Alaska, pausing once behind driftwood to regard me. At low tide the fox will find clams or other marine creatures that have washed ashore or become isolated in tidal pools.

Opposite: Although red foxes are very shy creatures, they may become tolerant and even curious of humans where they are not persecuted. This young one in Saskatchewan watched Peggy while being photographed by me.

Following spread: A red fox of the cross-phase hunts on a snow-packed landscape. Black-, cross-, and common red-color phases might occasionally appear in the same litter.

Opposite: All senses alert, an adult red fox is ready to pounce on its prey, maybe a mouse, which it cannot see clearly in the grass ahead.

Above: While driving through North Dakota, we spotted this family of red fox pups sitting above the entrance to their den (probably an enlarged prairie dog burrow). The animals were easily visible, not far from a fairly busy, paved highway.

Left: Family life around a northern swift fox den in Alberta. These foxes soon became accustomed to having a photography team in the vicinity, but did not venture too far from the safety of the burrow entrance. Not nearly as shy as their red fox cousins, they were almost eradicated by poisoning campaigns.

Right: This male swift fox kept mostly out of sight during broad daylight, setting out to hunt at dusk and returning at daybreak. Swift foxes live mostly by hunting small prairie rodents and ground-nesting birds. They have never been a nuisance to farmers or ranchers.

Below and opposite: The extremely shy kit fox of the Southwest is no easy species to observe or photograph during the day.

Opposite. Locally known as the cat fox, the gray is similar to the red fox in physique and silhouette, but its color is distinctive. The hunting ranges of gray fox pairs average smaller than those of red foxes, no doubt because of greater year-round availability of prey.

Above: Like all wild dogs, a hunting gray fox is a study in constant alertness and awareness of its surroundings.

Left: Unique among wild dogs, gray foxes are fairly good tree climbers, which gives them access to wild fruits before they fall to the ground, as well as to bird nests and their contents. This one has climbed into an old hollow stump. Grays often spend the daytime resting in hollow trees.

Above: These two gray fox pups are the boldest of the litter. Although their natural range is extensive, grays are most common in the southern half of the United States and in woodlands, not farming areas.

Opposite: A gray fox always blends well into its surroundings, but never more so than from September until all the leaves fall. Then its coat is the rich color of autumn.

Above: Especially during the short Arctic winter days, the white fox is a beautiful and mysterious wild dog, hunting and exploring its cold blue-and-white environment.

Right: Because of its thick, long-haired pelt, an Arctic fox gives the impression of being much larger than it is. Only about a foot high at the shoulder, an adult's average winter weight is only eight to ten pounds.

Above: Once when photographing a polar bear near the shore of Hudson Bay, an Arctic fox suddenly materialized beside the bruin. We wondered if this was the bear the fox would follow onto the freezing ice pack when winter arrived.

Left: These Arctic fox pups in their natal den beneath the tundra are only a few days old. Their eyes are still closed or just opening. Weighing only a few ounces, they are helpless.

Above: Not all Arctic foxes are always pure white. In summertime when the long hairs are shed even the white foxes are grayish. Others are gray or blue year-round.

Right: We located this den and litter of Arctic fox pups by watching where the mother had carried the carcasses of dead sea birds. These pups probably were not yet fully weaned and would only play with the carcasses, rather than eat them. The female barked incessantly the entire time we remained in the vicinity.

Above: By about five weeks of age Arctic fox pups are more lively and begin to explore a little beyond their dens. During this time, they are highly vulnerable to a long list of polar-region predators.

Left: Always a potential natural enemy, a predator of all young foxes in North America, is the great horned owl, which lives everywhere on the continent.

All of these are common, if not frequent, prey species of North American foxes. Red and Arctic foxes may depend heavily on Arctic ground squirrels or "siksiks" (above). Chipmunks (opposite, above) and cottontail rabbits (right) are eaten by all foxes except the Arctic foxes. Thirteen-lined ground squirrels (opposite, left) share the red fox's range in the eastern United States. Uinta ground squirrels are actively hunted by red foxes and coyotes, as are prairie dogs (opposite, right) in the West.

Above: Kittiwake and murre nesting areas like these in Alaska, attract both Arctic and red foxes for a short time each summer. The foxes eat eggs and nestlings.

Opposite and right: Blue foxes lurk at the foot of nearly vertical cliffs on Saint Paul Island, Alaska, where parakeet auklets and puffins nest. The foxes catch any hatchlings that fall or are pushed out of the nests. For a few weeks these birds are a steady source of food for the foxes.